MURDERER
At The Road Ranch

Sunset McGee figured he might spot some miscreant described on the Wanted posters on the stage bound for Buckskin at daybreak. The innocents he found instead—two pretty schoolteachers and a couple of drummers from the East—started more trouble than an ordinary guy could stir up, or an ordinary sheriff could handle.

When they started a fight at the road ranch, a quick-trigger hombre used the cover to disappear, and Deputy McGee wouldn't rest another sunset until he'd caught up with his man!

Also by W. F. Bragg:

MOUNTAIN MAVERICK
BUZZARD'S ROOST
GUNS OF ROARING FORK
RANGE CAMP
STARR OF WYOMING
TEXAS FEVER
BULLET SONG
SHOTGUN GAP
GHOST MOUNTAIN GUNS
BULLET PROOF
MAVERICK SHOWDOWN

BUCKSKIN RIDER

W. F. Bragg

LEISURE BOOKS   NEW YORK CITY

A LEISURE BOOK

Published by

Dorchester Publishing Co., Inc.
6 East 39th Street
New York, NY 10016

Copyright © MCMLVI by Arcadia House

All rights reserved. No part of this book may be reproduced or transmitted in any form or by any electronic or mechanical means, including photocopying, recording, or by any information storage and retrieval system, without the written permission of the Publisher, except where permitted by law.

Printed in the United States of America

CHAPTER I

SUNSET MCGEE STROLLED INTO HAPPY JACK Coogan's road ranch at daybreak. He had ridden in on his bay cayuse shortly after the arrival of the coach bound from Piute to Buckskin, a mining camp ten miles north. His tired pony was this moment munching a feed of oats in Jack's stable.

The Piute County deputy paused briefly in the doorway, running his eyes over the occupants of the long smoky room which was redolent with the smells of breakfast. He might spot some western miscreant wanted for a felony and described by one of the police folders stowed away in Sunset's saddle pocket.

At first glance he saw nobody of interest and his thoughts turned gratefully from duty to the pleasure of stowing away ham and eggs and coffee. It had been a thirty-mile ride from the county seat and Sunset had pulled his belt up to the last notch.

As he started to step from the door to the long counter where a Chinese cook laboured dishing out the morning meal, he noted idly two fat men who appeared to be salesmen. Both wore derby hats. One also wore a long white linen duster. Then Sunset's bright blue eyes gleamed at sight of two women who had just ridden in on the coach. One was young and sprightly, her companion a bit older yet demure and pretty.

Happy Jack's road house was built of pine logs with the bark on and gyp daubing to fill the cracks. The ceiling was lined with cheap white cotton sheeting which kept clods from falling to the floor from the dirt roof and muddy water from dripping in when it rained, which was seldom. This sheeting also served as a runway along which rattlesnakes quite often pursued mice and pack rats.

The cabin was divided into two rooms. The one into which Sunset walked was used as a bar and dining room. A plank bar ran along one wall, with a moon-faced barkeep in a collarless boiled bosom shirt as servitor. Although it was a treacherously early hour for whisky, he was serving drinks to a half-dozen cowpunchers who showed all the signs of a hard and sleepless night.

Sunset surmised that some cow outfit had paid off the day before and that the crew had pulled into Jack's for a seance of poker and liquor. A man could save money by blowing in here, since Jack's prices ran below those of Buckskin, the boom town.

The cook operated the lunch department across from the bar, another plank counter. A smoky kitchen was behind same, with worn stools for the customers. In addition to the coach passengers and Sunset, there were a half-dozen customers. From their gear a man couldn't say offhand what trade they pursued, if any.

Sunset recalled that once Happy Jack had operated the top restaurant in Buckskin. Then events had forced him to move ten miles from town. Some of these events were the reasons that had inspired Sunset to make his ride.

Two stools remained vacant in front of the lunch counter. Sunset and the male coach passengers held back politely while the two females, with much rustling of long dusty gowns, swung up on the high seats. They looked around for menu cards, but the cook chanted the breakfast bill of fare in melodious English flavoured with Cantonese.

"Likee eggee. Likee bacum. Likee hot cookie. All verry verry nice."

"Shirr mine, please," whispered the demure female. She wore a black costume: tight Basque style waist, sweeping black gown that hid her tiny toes, a sort of turban on her soft brown hair with a big red bird's wing pinned to it.

The Chinese blinked his liquid brown eyes and scratched his black pate. "All same fry, boil," he objected.

The second lady explained. She was wearing a dashing blue suit that seemed to defy the dust and sand of old Wyoming. When she swished around, her gown seemed to mold every graceful line of her sinewy, long-limbed figure. She was a golden blonde with black eyebrows, and she talked as though she had just swallowed a spoonful of wild honey.

"When you shirr 'em," she said in her rich succulent voice, "you put 'em in little moulds like cookies and bake 'em."

The cook grinned in open admiration but continued to scratch his head. He was an Americanized Chinaman, for he had cut off his pigtail and now barbered his locks by putting his head in a soup bowl and cutting around the edges.

"No bakee," he said. "Boilee. No bakee."

"All right then, friend. Deal 'em out to the both of us fried. Sunny side up."

"You bet. Deal 'em out damn quickee." And the Chinaman bobbed around to his big hot coal stove.

"He swore," object the lady in the black garments.

"Now, Mildred," answered the blonde, "that was just his way of speaking. No harm intended. Remember, now you are in the land of Adventure, the sunburnt West. You are enjoying morning in Wyoming. Massachusetts is far beyond the eastern skyline."

"Massachusetts is a good little old state," whispered demure Mildred, "a good place to hail from, Dulcy."

"You bet," approved Dulcy, twinkling her blue eyes under the arching pencil-thin black brows. "Better to be from than in. Me for Wyoming." She gave a little musical whoop. "Buckskin or bust!"

Sunset stood near the entrance waiting for the ladies to be served. He couldn't help but hear their remarks. Their cheerful patter amused him. They would need all their cheerfulness to get through a spasm of Buckskin, he opined. When Dulcy whooped, one of the cowboys over at the bar raised up, whipped out a long gun and roared hoarsely, "Buckskin or bust!"

Then he swung his back to the bar and, lining his gun, shot a neat hole through the top of Sunset's high-crowned cream-coloured fourteen-dollar Four X beaver Stetson hat.

His five friends eyed this target practice with nodding approval. The fat barkeep clamped his teeth down savagely on the butt of a black cigar stub.

The drummer who wore the duster dived behind the cigar counter at the end of the bar. The other, a chubby fellow who wore a black derby hat, stood his ground.

At the sound of the gunshot, the cook dropped an egg and broke it on top of the stove instead of in the frying pan. He jumped and grabbed the pan and whirled around with a terrible curse that would require a translator skilled in high-style Mandarin.

The little woman called Mildred, the one from Massachusetts, screamed in a voice like a cello and tried to climb over the lunch counter. The blonde Dulcy seized a bottle of catsup, gripped it by the neck, whirled around on her stool, then set her high heel solidly on the dirty floor.

The gunman, still lounging with back to the bar, threw back his head and whooped again, "Buckskin or bust!" And then he gave Sunset the evil eye. "When you come in here, take off your hat! Bow your head and raise your voice in praise to Buckskin and its peerless boss, Big Freddy Firebank."

Five of the barflies nodded solemnly, pounded on the bar, and echoed the yell: "Hurray for Big Freddy Firebank!"

But Sunset noted that the sixth, far along the bar, did not join the cheering section. This individual was a long lean grey-faced man, clad in dusty grey nondescript garments. Even the dust on his boots looked a duller grey than could be found in most alkali flats in Wyoming. He had merely swung around solemnly when all the fun began and was watching Sunset with a dull grey glare.

Sunset didn't reach up to take off his hat. So there were but five to face. The grey man wasn't numbered with the Big Freddy reception committee. The cheerleader was a broad-beamed, scaly scamp. He reminded Sunset of an outsized horned toad, except that he sported a bushy red moustache as tangled and spiky as a coil of rusty barbed wire. Sunset had never seen a horned toad with a moustache.

The fat drummer in the black derby hat standing just a few feet from Sunset whispered from the corner of his mouth, "What's the matter with these fools—shooting a hole in a man's hat just because he wears it into this dirty joint?"

"My good friend," drawled Sunset, turning bright blue eyes on the fat drummer, "and I certainly hope you will soon prove to be, I believe we have run into some sort of a civic committee from Buckskin. They revere the very name of that western paradise. They bow down too—and they believe all others should— to the name of their great man, fearless Freddy Firebank, the big boy of Buckskin!"

The horned toad spoke again and quite angrily to Sunset. "Didn't you hear me admonish you just now? Take off your hat and bow to the name of Big Freddy."

"First, my friend," Sunset said softly, and with a smile on his pleasantly homely face, "I must beg the disclosure of your name. If I bow to Big Freddy, surely I should give a nod to his valiant man-at-arms. So," and now sharply, "spit it out fast. What's *your* name?"

"You talk," growled the horned toad, "like you had swallered a Webster's dictionary. I suppose you are one of these eddicated sharps who wants to take over good old Buckskin and run a whizzer on us boys." He tilted his gun. "I am known far and wide as One-Eared Budge. And the next time I shoot, I will blow out your collar button."

For the rest of his life, Sunset wondered if Budge would have shot his head off his shoulders if not prevented. But that was not permitted to happen. Dulcy, holding her ground but quivering all over like a thoroughbred Kentucky filly after a close finish, snapped the catsup bottle from her white hand. It whipped through the air, making one complete turn, and hit Budge on the point of his bristly chin.

Budge rolled back his eyes, curled up his fingers, dropped his gun, and fell back over the bar.

His mates swung their eyes in amazed gaze first

to their felled leader, then to the defiant Diana in the swishing blue gown. She, for her part, had swung about and was reaching for the big tin pot of coffee which the Chink had previously planted on the lunch counter.

She spun around, kicking her gown aside with a high-heeled slipper. She swung the coffee pot around her head like a cowpuncher wafting a lariat noose.

"Buckskin or bust!" she cried in a thrilling voice.

Then she threw the pot.

Hot black Java liberally showered the aides of One-Eared Budge. One and all gave ground hastily, for steaming shirts were scorching their ribs.

"Gee Cli!" shouted the Chink cook approvingly. "Fine pitcher." And then he threw the frying pan.

This gave Sunset time to lurch across the room to the bar. While he pursued his way, he kept a weather eye cocked on Dulcy and the Chinese. They seemed sure of aim. But they were so whole-souled they might aim at any target that showed in their sights.

As Sunset lunged to the bar, One-Eared Budge awoke. His boots hit the dirt floor. He swayed a moment groggily. His pistol lay on the floor. He sighted Sunset and lashed out with a fist that scraped the side of the deputy's lean jaw.

Sunset landed a short right hook in return that smacked into Budge's left cheek. Budge broke at the knees. As he slumped to the floor, Sunset landed a straight right against Budge's gaping mouth. Budge went down in a bloody heap.

Jamming his back against the bar, Sunset faced Budge's followers. His knuckles bled where they had scraped against Budge's big teeth. His first thought then was to jerk his gun and end this shindig. For his opponents were armed. But he had been advised to handle business in Buckskin with tact. Therefore he defended himself with feet and fists.

Budge's limp body somewhat hampered the deputy's footwork but also interfered with the rush of the first man to reach Sunset. This fellow—lanky as a starved coyote and with a long twisted blue nose—tripped over Budge as he struck at Sunset with his gun barrel. Sunset gave him a knee in the middle, and Lanky howled and cursed and fell atop Budge.

The fat man in the derby hat bellowed, "Two down!" and came waddling toward Sunset with fists flying. Another of the Budge contingent promptly pounded the derby hat down over the drummer's face, blinding him, then hit him a glancing blow on the back of the neck with six inches of pistol barrel. The drummer reeled across the room, striving to pull his hat away from his eyes.

But in putting the drummer out of the battle, the pistoleer exposed himself to Sunset's attack. Stepping over the two writhing men on the floor, Sunset ducked under a wild swing and popped his fist up under the pistol whipper's left ear. The gunman spun around and staggered toward the lunch counter. Dulcy, who had been watching, bright-eyed, jumped nimbly aside. She laughed and whooped, "Buckskin or bust!"

Mildred from Massachusetts, who had now picked herself off the lunch counter, almost burst into tears. She cried out, "Dulcy, how can you?"

"Treat 'em rough!" laughed Dulcy, and kicked the pistol whipper in the ribs, putting him also out of the fight.

From the corner of his eye, Sunset caught the flash of trim leg and high-heeled slipper and approved deeply. There stood a girl to ride the river with.

There were now three of Budge's men down for the count. A fourth remained. He had not cared to blister his feet, or bang his fists against the tough features of Sunset. Instead, at a safe distance, he trained his pistol barrel on the narrow space between Sunset's blue eyes.

But before he could pull the trigger and interfere murderously with the coming of law and order to Buckskin, the lean grey man seated at the end of the bar jerked a gun with a motion as smooth as the cream of Jersey cow milk.

"Let's keep everything nice," drawled the grey gunman. "No wild bullets. There are ladies present."

CHAPTER II

SUNSET BLEW UPON HIS RED AND STINGING knuckles. Then he bowed gratefully to the bright-eyed Dulcy. "I thank you 'most to death," he told her gently. Then, turning to the grey man, he took off his hat for the first time that morning. "And to you," he went on, "the bow that was not vouchsafed to Budge and his boss and the glory of Buckskin!"

Then the smile of gratitude froze on Sunset's homely face and his eyes sharpened like diamonds.

"But why you'd wade in to save my hide," he went on, "beats me from soda to hock! Of all men in Piute County—Lonesome Luke himself. Lonesome Luke Suggs."

The grey eyes in Luke's long face became as hostile and dangerous as those of a trapped lobo wolf.

"The law," Lonesome Luke answered icily, "I wasn't worried about your hide none. But them ladies over there started this game, and I wanted to see 'em rake in the pot."

"That sentiment becomes you, Luke," Sunset said reflectively. "I can remember that it was not more than a week gone when my boss, the honoured sheriff of Piute County, ran you out of town with a gun."

"And you and six more gents backed up his play," said Luke.

"The sheriff said you were a reprehensible character. You had shot down a man in the Green Light who had the audacity to believe you had hidden a fifth ace up your sleeve."

"A character who gets fretful over a little old fifth ace," growled Luke, "ain't fitten for this world. He should have backed up his unkind thought by shooting before he wondered."

"Piute," drawled Sunset, "the pride of this county and the seat thereof, now glows with civic pride unclouded by careless gunsmoke. Which, my friend, caused the sheriff to desire that you abscond forthwith and darn quick. Which you did."

"Which I did, being outgunned in the premises."

"You are now heading for Buckskin."

"I aim to take a look at that camp. Any objections?"

"No objections," said Sunset. "But for you, I would not be in any position at this moment to object. I would be stretched out here with my good old friend, One-Eared Budge, with nobody to mourn my passing."

Ducly broke in brightly, "Buckskin or bust! Boysie, I would miss you."

Sunset and Lonesome Luke now gave their full regard to the ladies. Sunset recovered the frying pan and coffee pot and took the utensils over to the counter. He passed them to the cook.

"Deal these ladies from a fresh deck," he ordered.

"Damn right," said the cook, and turned gleefully to his hot stove.

For his part, Lonesome Luke tenderly lifted Mildred from Massachusetts into proper position on her stool, tried rather clumsily to brush off the hat with the red bird's wing. And while he thus ministered, Luke murmured, "You ladies sure are pure-strain, hundred per cent, copper-bottomed—"

"Now, Mister Luke," murmured Mildred, "you hush!"

Dulcy laughed merrily and called to her friend, "Isn't he a darling? Nothing like him in Boston!"

This drew the attention of the fat man, who had at long last removed his derby and punched out the dent in the crown. "Are you ladies from Boston?" he inquired in his thick wheezy voice.

"Mildred," said Dulcy, "comes from the Athens of America. As for me, I'm just a country girl."

This interesting talk was ended by the departure of Budge and his gang. Sunset stepped over and stopped the file of battered men before they reached the door. He ran a finger through the bullet hole in the peak of his hat.

"Fourteen dollars all shot up," he remarked. "Some gent has to make good."

Two of the boys were supporting Budge. The lanky man with the twisted blue nose was able to navigate under his own power. They listened sullenly to Sunset. He continued to smile. "Maybe," he suggested, "you'd prefer me to collect it the hard way."

At that they searched Budge's pockets, found a wallet and paid off Sunset. The barkeep assured Sunset they owed the house nothing. He would in fact pay money to get rid of their company.

The lanky man with the twisted nose growled to Sunset as he departed, "We'll see you again, stranger. In Buckskin."

Sunset grinned and watched them stagger outside, grope around the corner of the house toward a long hitchrack where some hip-slouched saddle ponies were tied. They had some trouble hoisting Budge into his saddle. When they departed, Budge was humped over the saddle horn as though he had taken aboard too much of Happy Jack's mountain lion tonic.

Sunset watched them go on down the long dusty road until they dropped out of sight over a sagebrush rise. He began to frown and scratch his head. There had been six at the bar, counting Lonesome Luke. That was his recollection. Then Budge and three men had joined in the attack.

He returned to the lunch counter and said to the breakfast guests, "One of that welcome committee turned up missing."

"That's right," said Lonesome Luke. He was seated alongside Mildred seeing that the Chinese cook supplied her with plenty of bacon and eggs. All the guests who had been there when the coach rolled in had departed. Only the two women and the two drummers remained of the coach contingent, and Sunset and Lonesome Luke.

Dulcy turned her lively eyes upon Sunset. "It seems to me that I did notice a man slip out the door while you were arguing with Budge."

Sunset wasn't worrying about this fifth man. The fight was over. But he asked, just to keep up the confab with this pretty girl, "What did he look like?"

She wrinkled her arched brows. "Nothing about him to remember. Just a nondescript character, one who'd not stand out in any crowd. Neither short nor tall, fat or lean." She narrowed her eyes again. "But there was something about him at that, if I could just remember."

"Thanks, Miss Dulcy. Not that we care a whole lot. But that lanky jaybird said I might meet up with 'em again in Buckskin."

The old stagecoach driver thrust his head through the doorway and yelled, "All aboard!"

As the passengers hurried outside, Dulcy lingered to say farewell to Sunset. "Let's hope we meet again in Buckskin."

"Buckskin or bust!" Sunset chanted softly. "That is my most fervent hope." Then as she flashed through the doorway, he called after her, "You have a mighty good throwing arm."

She gave him a last smile. "It comes in handy!" she called—and vanished. A moment later Sunset heard the rumble of wheels as the coach rolled away toward Buckskin. He gave his breakfast order to the cook, then sauntered over to the bar.

"What was the big idea of shootin' a hole in my hat?" he asked of the big black-haired barkeep. And then he went on. "And where's Happy Jack? Isn't like Jack to let a gang of hoodlum cowpokes take over his place."

The barkeep polished the bar. He favoured Sunset with a flash of sullenly dark eyes, then went on with his work. "They weren't cowpunchers," he growled. "They were some of Firebank's gang from Buckskin."

"I've heard of this Firebank lately but haven't crossed his trail. You know Firebank?"

"No. But I heard this Budge tell the rest before you walked in that a deputy sheriff named Sunset McGee was due in to sit on the Buckskin lid. I think Budge took a shot at your hat, hoping to tease you into a gun draw. Then they would've filled you full of lead and claimed self-defence."

Sunset thoughtfully considered the barkeep. There was something familiar about the blue-black jowls and dark staring eyes. "Buckskin has developed into a lively camp," he drawled. "They say there's a town election comin' up soon."

"Tomorrow, I heard. The toughs like Budge want to elect Firebank as mayor. They don't want no so-called honest citizen steppin' in to gum up their game." The barkeep bent and began to wash up pony glasses. "You did right well," he muttered, "but if you take my advice, you'll head back to Piute and keep away from Buckskin."

But Sunset wasn't through with the barkeep. "You haven't told me yet what became of Happy Jack. He's a good friend of mine."

"Well, you know they run Jack out of town. He was too honest for 'em. He shaped up as an opponent for mayor against Firebank."

"So Jack had to move here to make a living. But you haven't said yet where he is this minute."

The barkeep raised his head and said in a vastly irritated tone of voice. "I don't know what become of him. I came on shift just before daybreak. The place was open and Budge and his gang inside. Jack wasn't around. He said yesterday he might take the night off and go to Buckskin to settle some business."

"You said you don't know Fred Firebank?"

"No. I haven't been here long myself. Never yet got to Buckskin."

"There was a fellow with Budge's gang who sneaked out when the fight started. You remember him? He might have been Fearless Freddy."

"He was sort of an ordinary-lookin' hombre. I didn't pay much attention to him." The barkeep frowned, then added slowly, "Seems to me there was a little blue mark high on his right cheek. You'd hardly see it except in a strong light. Cheeks rather red, too, like he'd ridden in a frosty wind. But that's about all I remember. I was right busy seein' that that gang laid out their money for their fun."

Sunset quit the surly barkeep and sauntered over to his waiting breakfast. The cook could turn out a tasty dish of ham and eggs. When Sunset asked about Happy Jack, the cook said he hadn't seen his boss since coming on duty.

Before Sunset went to the barn to saddle up, he noted that Lonesome Luke had also departed. The man had not come in with the coach. Sunset surmised that Luke had put his saddle horse in the barn for a feed and rest, then mounted to follow the coach on its last lap into Buckskin. He had become vastly interested in Mildred.

"I might want to talk to you again about the Firebank gang," Sunset said before he went to the stable. He had lingered by the bar. "What's your name?"

The barkeep frowned, then growled, "Jones."

Sunset laughed as he left the bar. The barkeep didn't show much imagination. There were at least fifty men named Jones on the Buckskin range, most of them wanted by some sheriff. A camp like Buckskin drew outlaws the way sugar lures flies.

As the deputy sauntered into the barn, he was reflecting how a sudden mining boom had changed Buckskin from a peaceful little western trading post into a headquarters for outlaws and crooks. A few placer claims had been opened on the creek that gave its name to the camp; a discovery of gleaming golden dust and nuggets. It was enough gold to start a stampede and turn Buckskin overnight into a roaring hell on earth. The time would come when the gold would play out, the outlaws would move on and the eager-eyed boomers with them. But until that time came, men like Happy Jack would suffer, like old old-timers who had been there making a peaceful living until the boom struck.

Sunset pulled his saddle and bridle off a wall peg and moved down the dim centre aisle to lead out his bay pony. Only ten more miles remained of his long trip. Then—if Firebank's bunch didn't interfere—he'd unkink the knots of hard riding from his lean frame, eat a square meal, and take time to look into the camp situation. His face brightened, too, at the thought of helping the two schoolmarms to establish the first school in the tough camp.

He hoped the girls would not be interfered with by the lawless. Of course a decent citizen like Happy Jack, if elected mayor, would support their efforts. Sunset hoped that this election violence would die out. His boss had told him to sit on the camp lid without too much gunplay or fighting.

With his mind intent on happy thoughts on the future education of Buckskin's young, Sunset reached his mount's stall. Then he froze in his tracks, almost dropped saddle and bridle to reach for a gun. He thought instantly of the ordinary-looking man who had vanished from the bar as the fight began, and of Lonesome Luke.

Luke had no love for the law.

A hoarse voice wheezed, "Don't get fretful, friend. It's just me."

And out of the gloom waddled the fat drummer who had tried to help him in the fight. He was still wearing his dented derby hat and—in addition—

was now also wearing a white linen duster. Sunset recalled that the other drummer had worn a duster when he stepped in for breakfast.

Sunset eyed the fat man warily. "How come you missed the stage?" he asked.

The fat man came nearer, and Sunset saw that he carried a stubby pistol gripped in his right hand.

"I gathered from what I heard at breakfast that you were a sheriff's deputy," the drummer said in his throaty voice. "An officer of the law."

"Yes. What then?"

"So am I. Name's Charley McBatt. I hail from Boston, same as that teacher named Mildred. I am out here in your country trying to find a man."

"What for?"

"Murder!" McBatt blinked his hard eyes, waiting for Sunset to speak. When the latter remained silent, he went on. "I was sent out as sort of a private detective—although I hold rank in the Boston police department. I am on leave of absence to see if I can find this man. I wanted to talk to you, so I let the stage go without me. I thought I might talk to you here in the barn in private."

Sunset relaxed and smiled, glancing at Boston Charley's bulldog pistol. "You sure gave me a start. But you helped me against Budge and his gang. I want to thank you for that."

"I did what I could. If it hadn't been for my derby hat—" Then he shrugged and pointed toward the wooden oat bin where Jack stored his valuable horse feed. The door was padlocked. Sunset frowned. From beneath the door there was spreading a sticky dark pool.

Boston Charley pointed to it. "That looks like blood," he drawled. "I saw it here just before you stepped in. So I thought we'd check on it."

CHAPTER III

SUNSET BENT OVER AND INSPECTED THE STAIN closely. The light was poor here in the stable. Then he stared thoughtfully at the padlock closing the door. The bin was a large box, wide and high enough for a man to step inside and fill up a bucket of oats.

"That's what made me ask about Jack in the bar," he said to Boston Charley. "I rode in after the coach got here. I put up my horse. I hollered around for Jack or his hostler, for they generally have this bin locked. When I got no answer, I stepped down here and saw that the door was not locked. The padlock was open and hanging in it but hadn't been closed. I stepped in then and got my oats, figuring to find Jack later and pay him."

"I wonder who else has a key besides Jack."

"If that's blood," snapped Sunset, "it is still oozing out from beneath the door. Budge and his gang came out here to raise ned with Jack and his place. There's no time now to find a key."

Jerking his gun, he rammed the barrel against the lock and shattered it with a bullet. Then, opening the door, he peered into the dark room where the oats were stored. He felt Charley's breath on his neck and heard the Boston man whisper as he peered over Sunset's shoulder, "No sign of life in there. But it's dark."

Sunset bent forward. He drew in his breath sharply. Then he snapped to Charley, "On the floor. Don't you see?"

"See what?"

"The body of a man. All crumpled up."

Very gently the two officers carried the limp body out of the dark bin and stretched it on the hoof-marked boards of the barn centre aisle. Sunset stared down into closed eyes under dark brows. He looked up into Boston Charley's frowning face and shook his head.

"A friend of mine," he whispered. "Happy Jack Coogan. Owner of this road ranch. And—from what I heard—mentioned as a candidate for mayor of Buckskin."

"Is he dead?" Charley asked.

"No," Sunset answered. He had knelt and opened Jack's shirt to feel for a heartbeat. There was a feeble flutter. He rapped out a sharp command. "Hustle to the house. Get Jones and the cook and a bottle of whisky, and something to tote Jack on."

After Charley had hurriedly departed, Sunset made a closer inspection. Jack had been beaten viciously on the head. Blood oozed from a deep wound, staining his collar. There were other red marks upon Jack's sleeves, marks resembling red fingerprints as though he had been held on his feet before being pushed backward into the bin.

Sunset tentatively rubbed one of these marks with his fingertips. It was not blood. He stared down at it. His fingertip was stained as though tinted with red barn paint. But Jack's barn was not painted that colour.

The arrival of help for Jack made him dismiss the mysterious red marks from his mind for the time. A shot of whisky forced between Jack's lips made the road ranch owner shiver. Then he opened his eyes. He stared up into the deputy's face. His eyes were dull and glazed, and when Sunset called the man's name there was no response.

"He's stunned," Sunset said sadly. "He may never come out of it."

"Skull fracture or concussion," Charley judged.

The cook moaned, "That Freddy gang killee good boss man."

"He's not dead yet," Sunset said sharply. "Get the wagon tarp. We'll carry him into the house."

"Who beaned him?" asked Charley.

"Might be this Firebank gang. They had already run him out of town. He wanted a clean camp. So they came out to wreck his place, jumped him, maybe hit him too hard when he fought. Coach maybe came up too quick. Interrupted the beating—"

"So then while the fight was goin' on in the house, somebody slipped out—"

Sunset finished for him. "That fifth man sneaked out here and really knocked Jack cold. He dragged him into the bin and snapped the padlock. Wanted time to get away."

"Strange they'd take time then to lock up."

"Figured it might delay anybody who saw the blood running from under the door. The bin was probably open while Jack was doin' barn chores before the coach got in. They knocked him out then and laid him in a stall. Whatever they did, Jack wasn't in the bin when I put up my horse. For I tried to find him to pay for my oats. The bin was unlocked then."

A search revealed the padlock key in Jack's pocket.

"Which proves Jack had opened the padlock before he got jumped," said Sunset. It proved also that Jack had been stowed in the bin after Sunset put up his pony,

BUCKSKIN RIDER 27

about the time the fight had started in the barroom.

"I can account for four of that gang," growled Sunset. "But there was this fifth man. An ordinary-lookin' hombre, so Dulcy and the barkeep thought. A man who wouldn't stand out in a crowd." He frowned. "The barkeep said this fellow had a little blue scar high on his right cheek, but one you'd hardly notice except in a bright light. Fellow looked red, too, like he'd been riding in a hard wind. Otherwise—nothing."

Sunset turned to the others. "No way here to help Jack. We must get him to Buckskin."

"Is there a doctor in that camp?" asked Jones, the barkeep.

"Not a regular sawbones. A horse doctor named Backhammer. But he's right good with horses. I figure he can help Jack."

"Never heard of him," said Jones, "but then I just got in a week ago from down around Laramie." He eyed Jack gravely, then shrugged. "Reckon my job's played out. I'll move on."

"But somebody has to look after Jack's place here, feed the barn stock and see that coach passengers get fed each day."

"I didn't come up here to mix in no fights, friend. That Firebank gang may suck me and the Chink into this thing next. No—I reckon I better move on."

Sunset's first angry impulse was to put his gun on Jones and order him to stay on the job. Then he recalled his chief's advice to use diplomacy in keeping the lid of the law tightly shut over Buckskin. He sighed and turned to the cook. "You keep an eye on your boss while I hunt up a team in the barn."

"I'll help," said Boston Charley.

As Sunset led out the door, he turned for a last time to Jones. "I reckon you wouldn't reconsider?" he coaxed. "After all, you'd be helpin' out law and order."

Jones showed his big white teeth in a sneer. "To hell with law and order," he growled.

Sunset's face reddened. Boston Charley grinned sardonically at the frowning Jones. "Hurray," the Boston agent cried softly. "Buckskin or bust!"

But when they were in the barn, Sunset said to Charley, "We can't put that poor cook up against the blaze by leavin' him here all alone. We got to find some way of persuading Jones to guard the joint."

"I don't like the way Jones talks," agreed Charley, "but there's no way of keeping him on this job. Of course he'll have trouble getting out. No horse. Have to walk."

"He could camp down the road and catch the coach goin' into Piute today," Then Sunset turned to his saddle which hung on a peg. He grinned at Charley. "There's more than one way," he drawled, "of skinnin' a cat."

From a saddle pocket, he extracted a roll of paper folders. Charley watched impatiently. He was anxious to hook up a team and get on the road with Jack.

Sunset knelt and deliberately spread out the folders. One by one, he inspected them quite closely. Boston Charley frowned and bent nearer. "Why," he growled, "these are reward notices and the like sent out by police departments and sheriffs. Wanted men."

"Yeah. Wanted men. I call this collection my travelling library. Now here, for instance, is a gent that is almost a dead ringer for that Lanky with the blue nose. One I kicked in the middle. You remember Lanky?"

Now Charley also knelt and inspected the folder passed to him.

"Reward of five hundred dollars hung on him," he read off. "Wanted by the Sweetwater County law for killin' a rancher over a stolen horse. He's known as Slim Osage down there. But this describes our friend Lanky even to his twisted blue nose. Says, too, he goes armed and is dangerous." Charley laughed. "Well, bud, looks like you'll make yourself five hundred dollars if you live long enough to pinch Slim."

"Ain't supposed to accept rewards," said Sunset.

He was intently ruffling through the remainder of folders. Finally he grinned and passed one to Charley. "This'll do to hold him," he suggested.

Charley read it and nodded. "Another fat reward," he said. "A thousand bucks offered by the Laramie law for Rattlesnake Bill Jay. It's our friend, Barkeep Jones, to the life, even to the big black moustache."

"Another killer," said Sunset.

"But this time they stood face to face and Rattlesnake took a slug through his left arm to down his man. I thought that was self-defence out here."

"Probably other reasons why Laramie wants him," said Sunset.

"What do you figure to do? If you arrest Jones—or rather Rattlesnake Bill—you'll have to take him with you to Buckskin. That way, this road ranch will be left unguarded except for the cook."

Sunset nodded. He looked thoughtful as he folded up his library of crooks on the run and stuffed it into his saddle pocket. "Have somehow to get the best of

Rattlesnake," he murmured. "But now let's get a team hooked up. I saw a buckboard out in back here."

So a frisky team was hitched to Jack's buckboard. Hay was put in the box for softening under blankets and quilts. Jack was lifted up and placed in the box. Then Sunset saddled up his bay horse.

"I'll drive," he said to Charley. "You ride and sorta keep your eyes peeled."

Boston Charley inspected Sunset's bay pony with a dubious eye. "I had intended to hire a pony and ride to Buckskin with you," he confessed. "But to tell the truth, I never had much to do with horses before."

"He looks tough but he's plumb gentle. Just don't kick him in the ribs."

"What do you call him?"

Sunset grinned. "You'd blush to hear what I call him when he acts ornery. But his regular name is Sooner because he'd sooner eat than work. You get aboard him, Charley, and treat him right, and he'll carry you from here to Montana without wettin' a hair of his hide."

Jamming his derby down on his head and buttoning his duster tightly around his portly form, Charley approached the pony. "I will try anything once," he declared.

"If you didn't aim to ride a pony," said Sunset, "you should have stayed on the coach."

Charley gave him a wink. "But I wanted to talk to you in private. You know what for."

Jones and the cook had lingered after the stowing of Jack in the buckboard. Jones eyed the Boston man. "Right queer how you were in that barn when Coogan was found." He pondered deeply, then added,

"This Lonesome Luke, too. He drifted away on the quiet."

Charley laughed. "I hope you aren't thinking that I conked Jack. Why would I jump him? I'm just a drummer hitting this country for the first time, out to open new territory."

"I didn't hear you say what you were peddlin'," Jones asked. "If Jack ever gets well, I got pay coming. I might be interested in your line. What is it? Jewellery, cigars or the like?"

Charley laughed. "My trunk went on to Buckskin with the coach. I'll pick it up there. I sell a line of patent medicine called Peerless Painkiller. Good for most of the common aches and pains—sour stomachs, gallstones, hollow teeth, fever and ague."

The cook patted his round stomach. "I likee buy some of your Painkillee. Belly feel bad after fight."

Charley shook his head. "All my stock went to Buckskin with the coach."

Sunset cut in. "We got to get Jack to Buckskin for help. You stay here, cook."

But the cook frowned and shook his head. "Stomach feel bad. Go to Buckskin with Jack. Take some of this Painkillee." He turned toward the eating house. "I got to get hat and coat."

The barkeep laid a heavy right hand upon the cook's shoulder and spun him around. "You can't quit that way," he growled. "Jack's been good to you."

"I know," the cook said indignantly. "I go 'long, take care of Jack. He my good friend. But my belly, he hurt too." Then he asked, "How come you want me for stay? You say you quit. You 'fraid?"

Sunset eyed the barkeep smilingly. "I don't think

Jones is afraid. It's true his left arm bothers him some. I see him go easy with it when we lifted Jack into the buckboard. But down Laramie way, the folks say Jones is not easily scairt."

The barkeep frowned, then thrust his right hand under his sagging vest. But he desisted when he found himself staring into the barrel of Sunset's gun.

CHAPTER IV

"DOWN AROUND LARAMIE," SUNSET WENT ON, "they say that Rattlesnake Bill Jay is fast on the draw except when he's been marked up by a hot slug."

Jones drilled the smiling deputy with his hard black eyes. His right hand remained half hidden under his vest.

"If you're packin' a hideout gun, forget it," said Sunset. "You try to use it and I'd be forced to shoot you in the right arm. They already got you pinked in the left. And that would knock you out as a barkeep. For a barkeep who can't use both hands is a pathetic sight indeed."

"My name is Jones and my left arm's all right."

"You didn't try very hard when we were lifting up Jack."

"I tell you—" Jones began sullenly. But before he could finish, the Boston detective stepped in and punched Jones lightly in the left arm. Jones flinched and cursed. Sunset and Charley laughed. Then Sunset explained. "There's a thousand dollar reward on you, Bill. You wanted to quit. You figured to head for Piute. Instead—you are going to Buckskin with me. You are now under arrest for murder."

"You are abducting me," complained Jones.

Sunset laughed. "No—I am familiar with your homely features, Bill. And we have word about you from the Laramie County sheriff. You are classed as a tough old boot who'd rather kill than eat."

"They got me pegged wrong. I'm a peaceful character. Just a cowpoke off the Medicine Bow range. If they list me as a killer, they lie. It was self-defence."

"That's what they all say," said Boston Charley.

Unwillingly the burly barkeep removed his gun hand from under his coat. "I haven't got a hideout gun," he said indignantly. "Don't believe in 'em. I was just scratchin' myself. I always get scratchy and nervous when a sudden deal comes up like that you just sprung on me."

A cold little wind was blowing out of the west across the brown bare badlands. The Chinese cook and Boston Charley shivered. But never a tremor shook Sunset or Rattlesnake Bill.

"You know, Bill," Sunset rattled on brightly, "a lot of men have been mowed down for feeling itchy and reachin' under their coats in moments of dire extremity."

Bill showed his big white teeth in a brief chilly grin. "You talk like you had swallowed a dictionary. You go in for big words, don't you?"

"I always pack a library with me wherever I go. Time passes swiftly when you got interesting subjects to ponder over."

Bill relaxed. "Now me," he drawled, "I'm different from you. I know what lots of big words mean but I can't pronounce 'em. But you—"

"What are you drivin' at? I can pronounce lots of big words but don't know what they mean. Is that it?"

"Yeah."

Sunset continued to smile just as frostily as Bill. "I know what murder in the first degree means," he said gently. "I can pronounce it all. And, Bill, so can you. I pegged you in one little book of my library published down in Laramie. And so—"

"I told you," Bill went on, never batting an eye, "that I never carried a gun under my arm. But you can't blame a man for—" And suddenly he had dropped his right hand and thrust aside the front of his coat. His fingers curled around the stock of a gun which he had thrust down behind his waistband. It was a deadly fluid attempt at a quick draw. Cold-nerved, too, standing as Bill did under Sunset's gun.

But the deputy, laughing icily, snapped down the barrel of his gun, struck Bill's hairy right wrist a smart tap. Bill's fingers popped apart. Then his right hand dropped limply to his side.

"Be good, Bill," Sunset admonished. "I figured a dead game sport like you would have an ace in the hole somewhere."

"You've numbed the big nerve in my arm," growled Bill. "Go ahead and shoot. I can't resist. There's a thousand dollars blood money on me. Here's your chance to collect easy."

Sunset shrugged, said to Charley, "Get his gun and go over him for more iron." Charley obeyed, first taking away the long forty-five Bill carried. It was a beautifully balanced weapon of dully glinting blue steel. Charley deftly ran his hands over Bill, then said to Sunset, "He's clean now."

"Step around behind me," said Sunset. "There's steel cuffs stickin' out of my hip pocket."

Charley extracted the bracelets and came around Sunset. He stood waiting between the deputy and the cornered outlaw. Yum, the cook, round-eyed, had moved off a dozen steps out of possible bullet line.

"Stick out your mitts, Bill," Sunset ordered.

Bill licked his lips. His black eyes flashed under glowering bushy brows. "Supposin' I don't. What'll you do then?"

"Charley here knows how to handle cuffs. He can put 'em on yuh."

"If I fought him off that would give you an excuse to kill me. And the two of you would split a thousand bucks between you."

"Yum, over there, would be a witness against us."

Bill laughed nastily. "Chinks have been killed before. One bullet would shut up Yum."

"Yum's sick now. Look at him, Bill. Face green and eyes bulgin'. He sure needs Painkiller."

Sunset's easy drawling tone proved too much for Bill's curiosity. He turned his head slightly to glance at Yum. In that instant, Charley leaped like a tiger. The cuffs went clickety click. Bill raved and cursed. but he now wore the bracelets of the law.

"A plumb dirty trick," he snarled. "cuffin' me when my head was turned."

"Dirty tricks are all right against dirty killers," Sunset pointed out.

Enraged, Bill lunged forward, attempting to strike down Sunset with the chain drawn tautly between the gleaming cuffs. As Sunset stepped back, Boston Charley thrust his burly body between captor and captive and rammed the barrel of his bulldog pistol an inch deep into Bill's heaving paunch. Bill relaxed and a bitter grin curled his lips.

"Put up your toy gun," he said to Charley. "I know when I'm well beat. But you can't close my mouth unless you shoot me. I've been framed by the law down there. I was punchin' cows up along the

Buckskin River near this joint. Came to town to spend a little easy money I earned hard. Got into a card game. Some slick sports in it. Ran in a crooked deck. Dealer was named Mose DeBose. He had a pard in the place, but I didn't know it then, he was such an ordinary-lookin' sport. Anyway, when I called Mose it was a fifty-fifty break. I got my iron goin' first. Shot down Mose while he had a gun in his hand. But this pard of his goes to work with a little old sleeve gun, one of these two-barrel derringers. Got a gold ace of spades on it. I see it flash as he jerks it. By then I'm headin' out of there. Unexpected, he scratches my left arm with one of those little old bullets. Lames me some. But I got out and to my pony."

"Why did you run?" Sunset asked. "You say it was self-defence."

"I hid out to see what would happen. Friend comes ridin' along. Said the gang had hid out Mose DeBose's gun. And the dead man's pard had gone too, with his little old ace of spades derringer. What else could I do? I was just a busted cowpoke with a sore left wing."

"It's right late now for talking," said Sunset. "Time to talk to the law was right after you killed DeBose."

"They dug up a half-dozen witnesses from that card joint so say Mose wasn't armed. No mention was made of the pard with the derringer."

"You had a bullet crease along your left arm. That was a fact. If you had showed that to the sheriff, the law might have protected your interests."

Bill sneered. "The law has just done a fat job protectin' poor old Jack here. No—if you hadn't showed up with your friend—I had plans for protectin' myself. I was tipped off there was a connection between the gang runnin' that joint down there on Buckskin River and this gang up here in this other Buckskin. So I slipped up here on the quiet, hopin' to nose around and maybe overtake the man who packed the ace of spades pistol."

Sunset frowned. "How about that gang you were serving this morning? There was a fifth man you spoke of. Little scar on his face? Red cheeks?"

Bill looked baffled. "That's what I am up against. I never did get a good look at DeBose's pard. He was one of these fellows who wouldn't stand out none. He wasn't in the card game. He just stepped out after I shot down Mose. I was headin' fast through the back door. There was just this flash of gold from his little gun as he launches out. Then his slug nails me. By that time I'm outside and goin' fast for my pony."

"If you don't know him, how'll you overtake him?"

"My main hope is to find that little old ace of spades pistol."

Sunset sighed. "Well, since we got to take Jack to Buckskin for help, I reckon you must come along."

Bill laughed. "I won't last long in Buckskin. Not chained up. That pistol man knows me even if I don't know him. For all I know, he might be this fifth fellow you blame for bashin' in Jack's head."

Sunset nodded. Then he pushed back his hat and scratched his red head.

"What you want most of all in the world is to somehow find the pard of Mose DeBose and his trick gun?"

"Yeah. I never was an outlaw before this. I hate to chase around like a mangy coyote. Before I got into this trouble. I always tried to run a square game."

"You're still not sure you'd know the man who marked you up down there at the scene of demise of Mose DeBose."

"Now take it easy on that language, Perfessor. You mean at the scene of Mose DeBose's wipin' out."

"The same."

"I told you before he would pass in any crowd without attracting too much attention."

"The fifth man was like that."

"Yeah. He didn't say much. That big hombre, Budge, did all the loud talkin'. I'd bet that Budge cracked Jack on the head."

"Budge was inside with the others durin' the fight. I came in from puttin' up my pony and findin' the bin open. Durin' the fight this fifth man slips out. Budge and the rest ride away later. We watch 'em go. None of 'em goes to the barn. Then me and the drummer here—we find the bin locked and Jack inside. Since this fifth man was with the Budge gang, we have to assume it was him slipped out and really wound up Jack's clock while there was time."

Charley broke in briskly. "You know, Bill, with your reputation, if Sunset and the cook and me wasn't here to talk for you, folks might think *you* cracked down on Jack."

Bill cursed and fumed that Charley was locoed. Charley interrupted him.

"You are a killer on the loose," he said. "Folks imagine plenty things about killers on the run. They might say that Jack recognized you and wanted the reward, so you tried to shut him up and got interrupted."

"But I didn't knock out old Jack, I tell you." Bill became wildly angry. He waved his cuffed hands in the air. Only the threat of Sunset's gun prevented him from throwing himself upon Boston Charley. "Why," he yelled, "the cook *knows* I wasn't out of the house long enough to pound in Jack's head and hide him. The cook'll tell you. And Jack, too, when he gets back his senses."

"Maybe that nondescript fellow knows you now, Bill. Maybe they are framing you again," Sunset suggested. "You'll have the Chinaman on your side. But there'll be four or five to talk against you—all those members of the Fearless Freddy gang."

Bill glared around desperately like a wounded grizzly at bay. Then suddenly his head drooped and he let his locked hands fall limply in front of his body. "There's no justice," he groaned. "None at all for a simple-minded hombre like me. If Old Jack could just open his eyes and speak—"

Sunset took a key from his pocket with his left hand. He passed it to Charley. "Take off the cuffs," he ordered.

Charley's mouth dropped open in amazement. "Wha-what?" he stammered. "He's a killer."

"Take 'em off," snapped Sunset.

Charley gripped the cuff key in his hand. He frowned and stared into Sunset's unsmiling face. Then he shrugged fat shoulders and said coldly, "Sagebrush law is different from that in Boston."

"We all live to learn," murmured Sunset. "Take 'em off of him, Charley."

"Okay, bud. But remember I advised against it."

Rattlesnake Bill stood free, glowering at Sunset. "Now don't think you're softening me up," he rasped. "I still say the devil with your law."

"But you were just declaiming about justice. You said

there *wasn't* any. Well, here's a little sagebrush justice."

"I suppose you'll free me so that if they do jump me in Buckskin, I'll have a fightin' chance for my life."

Sunset grinned. He used his left hand to pull Bill's gun from behind his waistband. He handed it, barrel first, to the outlaw. Bill blinked his eyes. His deep frown seemed to cut gashes in his leathery face. "You—you're handin' over my gun," he stammered. "And me—me with a thousand bucks reward on me—"

"I figure," Sunset stated evenly, "like you, that your best show is to stay around here and somehow try to find that man who packs the gold-marked derringer. I can't be bothered guardin' you the next few hours in Buckskin. You're only ten miles out here, Bill. So I am askin' you to stay here for a day, take care of this place for Jack. In return for that, you'll later be a free agent in takin' the trail of the ordinary-looking hombre with the ace of spades pistol."

Boston Charley stood listening. His chubby face was unsmiling. His features looked as though they had been carved out of pink granite. He gave Sunset a long cold look, then turned his chilly glare on the big rawboned outlaw.

Bill stood staring down at the loaded gun which had been passed to him. He reversed it, curled his fingers around the polished stock. The limpness administered by the tap of Sunset's gun barrel had gone. He shifted the gun barrel slightly. The front sight came up almost in line with the top silvery button on the front of Sunset's overalls.

Boston Charley gagged, then whistled through his nose. A low moan sounded from the side lines as Yum, the cook, sank to his knees and covered his eyes. But

Sunset stood his ground with a little smile on his face.

Rattlesnake Bill looked up into the deputy's eyes. He thrust his gun down back of his pants. "It's a trade," he said huskily. "But hurry back."

CHAPTER V

THE BUCKBOARD RATTLED ALONG THE BUMPY road to Buckskin. Sunset guided the team. Charley, who had decided at the last moment not to ride the bay, had tied Sooner to the tail gate. He rode beside the Piute deputy. Yum, the Chinese, knelt behind in the box, caring for the stunned Happy Jack now wrapped warmly in blankets.

"The road to Buckskin," Sunset commented, pointing his whip at the surrounding colourful badlands hills. "A long and weary one."

Charley merely grunted and shrugged his shoulders.

Sunset knew the reason. He had released an outlaw and put the man on his honour not to quit the range.

The buckboard rattled through a stretch of dry hills. They were streaked blue and red and yellow where ancient seas had once laid down shore lines. In this country, men had found rare minerals, also the stony bones of huge beasts mired down in prehistoric ooze millions of years before the gold boom hit Buckskin.

"Regular picture country," Sunset explained. "Nothing like it around Boston, I expect. That blue stuff is gumbo. Yellow is clay. That red is a sort of oxidized iron ore. None of it worth much. The gold's up around Buckskin. We should be there shortly. The coach is about an hour ahead of us makin' six miles an hour. We're doin' about the same—"

"Forget your mathematics and your lectures. That outlaw you freed might be trailing us this very minute."

"He said he'd stay. He give me his word. After all, he didn't do much except to—"

Boston Charley turned red. Then he burst out angrily. "All he did was to kill a man."

"He said he killed Mose DeBose in self-defence. You heard him."

"But that isn't what the Laramie sheriff wrote in that folder we read."

Sunset chirped up the buckboard ponies over a smoother stretch of red dirt road. The buckboard's speed increased past solemn brown picket-pin prairie-dogs on guard at the mouths of their burrows, past meadow larks rising high into the air with their cheerful songs. The sun was now a trifle above the gloomy blue mountains to the eastward, its rays beginning to reach a man's vitals. Sunset whistled his horses on and felt that despite the unholy doings of Man, the things of Nature somehow restored faith.

"Bill's an outlaw," he told Charley. "He stands right now at the point where he can turn from an outlaw into one of these murderous crooks you're so danged familiar with. His big complaint is that somebody made a fool of the law in his case. He moaned around that there wasn't no justice. Well—now he knows there's a little bit of justice if you keep huntin' for it."

Charley sneered. "Just because a boxheaded fool with a star on gave him back his gun and took the cuffs off his wrists."

"Charley, as an officer, you should know that law—and justice—presume a man's innocent until he's found guilty. Well—in the case of Bill—I presumed right from the start. Anyway"—he nodded back to Jack, "what else was there to do? That poor fellow laid out—maybe by the Buckskin gang. If we all started to town with him, they might swoop down and set fire to the whole works, put Jack out of business right. Well, I know now that if they try any swoopin' down, Bill will put up a dead game fight to drive 'em off."

"Back in Boston you'd be kicked off the force."

Sunset smiled and flourished his whip, first toward a lean coyote slipping over a nearby hill with wary eye on the buckboard, then toward a band of graceful antelope circling across the road. "But this here," he said cheerfully, "is not Boston. This here is ol' Wyomin'."

Yum, the cook, who had taken in most of the conversation with wise understanding, grinned and chanted, "Buckskinnee or bustee!"

"Hurray!" Sunset cut in softly.

"Bah," snarled Charley, and buried his double chin deep in his coat.

So another mile clicked off on the hardpan road for there had not been rain for the past six weeks and the gumbo surface was dusty and smooth. But let an inch of rain fall, and this same desert thoroughfare to Buckskin would become a quagmire with the coloured muck reaching to the knees of the ponies.

"Buckskin or bust!" changed Sunset. Then he added whimsically, "I wish I was a poet. I'd write a verse bringin' in that sweet refrain. You know," he turned his bright eyes on the eastern detective, "I've read about how most cowboys on the Texas Trail are poets. In any salooon you can hear the darnedest songs bein' sung to words all writ down by Texas cowboys. Now, here and there, I've met a lot of Texans. But so far," he looked sorrowful, "I haven't met any poets. They are all good boys, hard riders and so forth. But when it comes to the music of words—"

Boston Charley reared around and roared, red-faced, "Shut up! Words! Words! Words! That's all I hear from you. What sort of a misguided addle-pated limb of the law ever named you as depty? What kind of a dedicated dope—"

Sunset turned his head and listened in honest admiration. "Words?" he repeated. "Say, Charley, I just talk about 'em. But you—why, you really got 'em. Words—say—"

"Bah!" bellowed Charley. "Action's what counts. *Action*—"

And, as though to accent his shout, from up the road came a swift drumming sound that boomed hollowly on the hardpan. Boston Charley fell silent, glaring ahead. Sunset quit smiling, and forgetful of Jack, laid whip to the nigh horse. The buckboard wheels churned swiftly on toward a low sagebrush ridge.

"What's that ahead of us?" cried Charley above the noise of rattling wheels, beat of hoofs, and screeching of dried-out parts of the buckboard.

"A horse comin' fast!" barked Sunset. Then to his team, "Giddap, boys! Lay into your collars!" and again gave the willing ponies an encouraging taste of the whip.

"A horse?" Charley squinted his cold marbly eyes against the dust. "But I don't see no horse—"

"Keep poppin' your eyes! You'll see him come over that ridge ahead, directly."

"But why you puttin' the team to a run? You might hurt Jack."

"Jack's stunned. He don't feel nothing."

"Just the same, all this excitement over a running horse—"

Sunset shook out his reins. "In this country," he

barked again—and very grimly, "only tenderfeet run horses when there's no reason for it. That horse we hear is at the dead gallop. That means trouble!"

Then, as the panting buckboard team lurched and tugged up the side of the sagebrush slope, a horseman came over the crest on the high run. His long grey whiskers floated in the wind. He bore down swiftly on the oncoming buckboard. The gap between lessened. Now in the dust they saw that he was riding a horse without a saddle, but wearing harness. The rider had thrust his legs down through the traces to anchor himself to his mount.

For a moment it appeared that the rider's glary-eyed mount would charge straight down upon the buckboard. Sunset hastily made a sharp turn from the road, giving the rider the space of a rut for passing. But as he put on the brake and halted his team half out of the road, the rider reined into a skidding dusty halt. For a moment his excited lathered mount threatened to pitch. But the rider grimly checked any pitching by holding high his horse's head.

Boston Charley shouted hoarsely, "It's the coach driver!"

The next moment he found the reins in his hand and heard the snapped out order of Sunset: "Watch the team."

Leaping out of the buckboard, Sunset hurried to where the driver had reined down. "Jake," he cried, "what's wrong?"

The driver blinked down into Sunset's face. His features were masked by the dust of his fierce gallop.

"Held up my coach!" he gasped. "Other side of the ridge there."

"Robbed you?"

"Sure. I tossed down the express box."

"Why did you head back this way?"

"Figured you were nearer than Buckskin. You see those holdups killed one of my lead team to halt me. That was bad. A darned good horse." And Jake wiped out his eyes. "But killin' the horse wasn't the worst. They went after a plumb innocent passenger!"

Sunset thought of Dulcy and turned cold. But Jake hurried on, "It was that drummer in the linen duster. They made all the passengers get out. Then this skinny holdup grabs him and guns him. The drummer was dead before he could beg for his life. That blonde schoolmarm get mad and jumps the killer, even though his gun was still smokin'."

"He hurt her?"

"Naw." Jake frowned, then shook his head in puzzled fashion. "No, he just laughs and bends her over backwards. And danged if he didn't kiss her. And she—well, she goes limp all over in the sagebrush."

Sunset was beside himself with rage. He almost dragged Jake off his horse. "You," he shouted, "what were *you* doing all this time?"

"What could I do? There was two of 'em. Other one was standin' by the road holdin' a rifle on me. So then the killer, after he had kissed this blonde—"

"I mighta known it would be Dulcy," commented Sunset.

"He says to her that he'll see her again right soon. The other hombre yells somethin' about Buckskin or bust. Then they get aboard their ponies and ride off. I get down, figure the man in the duster is a goner. This blonde says she will look after him while I go for help." Jake frowned on Sunset. "It was her that recommended I come to you."

That made Sunset flush. So she had thought of him in her dire extremity.

"Get in and ride," he said to Jake. "Tie your horse behind. Or follow me!"

"I'll follow," growled Jake.

Dulcy greeted Sunset with stony calm. Her eyes were bright and hard, with no trace of tears. In the coach, Mildred from Massachusetts wept helplessly. Dulcy told Sunset that the two riders who had halted the stage by shooting one of the lead horses wore nothing that would make them stand out from the usual Western crowd. "Just boots, overalls, dusty blue flannel shirts and grey slouch hats."

"Their horses?"

"A black and a bay."

"Any brands? Or marks?"

Dulcy stood close to Sunset for he had found it necessary to put an arm around her so that she would not faint on his hands. He didn't want another swooning female mixed up in this grim business of blood in the morning light.

Dulcy didn't answer at once. She stood frowningly running her gaze over the coach, the dead coach horse in the traces, the rescue buckboard and its lathered team, old Jake and his mount.

"I am not up on brands," she said finally. She flushed. Her face was dusty but the red blood showed plainly in her cheeks. She shuddered. "You'll just have to excuse me for not making better use of my eyes. But that brute—that laughing brute with the red face—"

"Red face?" Sunset snapped.

"You asked me if I remembered anything. That's about all. This killer—when he bent over me—his face was red as though he had painted it. I presume it was red dust from the road. He had horrible brown eyes. I'll never forget those eyes—"

"Brown eyes are right common. But this red face?"

"Dust, I suppose." Then she widened her eyes. "Oh yes, there was something else. The gun he used on this poor man here. A little thing it was. There was gold on it, for it flashed in the sun when he drew it. He was wearing a vest."

"Yes. Go on."

"He put up his murder gun when I tried to jump on him. He was laughing. Why should he care? There was this other man to keep watch."

"So he put up this little gun with the gold on it?"

"Yes. He moved very swiftly when he handled that gun. So this vest he wore—when he took me in his arms—it flopped open. And I saw that he was wearing some sort of a leather sling under his left arm. And there was the little gun tucked away." She twisted her lips into a bitter sneer. "An itty bitty pistol with a gold mark on it, on the place where the hilt touches the barrel. You know."

He put his arm around her, for he saw that she was trembling. Her brave attempt to save the man in the linen duster had failed. Shock now swept over her. For a moment she leaned against Sunset and buried her golden head against his steady shoulder. After a moment he asked softly. "This gold mark?"

"Like something you see in a—in a deck of cards. A spade. Only gold. That's it. Like a golden ace of spades."

Listening intently, Sunset didn't hear the approach of

Boston Charley. Now the stocky detective burst out, "So Bill told the truth. There was this gold-marked pistol."

Dulcy stepped away from Sunset. "Who's Bill?" she asked.

"Never mind," Charley snapped. He talked rapidly to Sunset. "That drummer in the duster is dead. Bullet in the head. Never lived after it hit him. Poor devil. A sure case of mistaken identity."

"What do you mean?" Sunset rapped.

"They wanted *me*. They thought they were killing Boston Charley McBatt. I suppose they were tipped off I'd pose as a salesman and be wearing a white duster and a derby. Well, I took off my duster last night. But the other poor fellow—he didn't. If I'd been along— wearing my duster—they'd have killed both of us to be sure."

CHAPTER VI

WHILE THE DRIVER AND YUM WRAPPED THE limp form of the murdered drummer in a wagon sheet, and Dulcy ministered to the moaning Miss Mildred, Sunset drew Boston Charley off for a council of war. The time had come, he declared, to talk of many things. "That's from a book," he explained, "but what we're in now isn't wonderful like the book. This is plumb low-down dirt, killing a poor jasper for no reason at all. For you must admit, the linen duster deal don't stack up strong."

Boston Charley eased his chubby form down on a rock and sighed deeply. "I also read books," he explained. "And I know where that line comes from. But as you say," he glanced despairingly around him at the suddenly desolate and forbidding-appearing western desert, "this sure ain't Alice's Wonderland. No grinning walrus here to recite pretty poetry. Just cold blood and worse—" Suddenly Charley shuddered, and his firm jaw began to quiver. Before Sunset could bend hastily and put an arm around Charley's stout shoulders, the ordinarily hard-eyed Boston officer had almost broken into open weeping.

"That poor fellow," he whispered brokenly, wiping his eyes. "Why—he was just a little man trying to make a living. And me—me with my fool stunt of playin' the part of an honest salesman—I—I brought about his death."

"How were you to know?" Sunset consoled him. "Somebody tipped 'em off."

Charley cleared his throat and wiped the last moisture from his eyes. Again he was in full control of his emotions, again the relentless law dog from the east. "I might've figured I'd be tripped up," he confessed. "The man I'm after is a brutal killer. But he's smart, mighty smart."

"His name?"

"The one he's wanted under is Frank Flarity. I think it is just an alias. He probably has operated under a dozen names. He's smooth, that Frank. And cruel."

"If it was Frank gunned that poor drummer, I know that, Charley: that he's plenty cruel."

Charley then told briefly what he knew about this mysterious Frank Flarity. A Romeo sort of operator. He had suddenly appeared from the hazy west. He preyed on weak and lonely women, preferably widows with bank accounts. His speciality was interesting them in gold mines. He flashed picture rock before their dazzled eyes, bull quartz ore studded with glistening wire gold. Of course the rich ore never came from the claims he advertised. Most of the time, Charley said, these claims consisted solely of the fake certificates of mining stock which Frank gave to his victim in return for her bank account.

"Our information is that if he couldn't get their dough any other way," Charley went on, "he married 'em." He shook his head admiringly. "He was a smooth operator when it come to love or money." Then the detective's voice hardened and his eyes narrowed to slits. "But the last lady he victimised, apparently she got a little bit suspicious about her Romeo. About two months ago he killed her."

That startled Sunset. "Hey," he asked sharply,

"you mean we got a lady killer running loose in Piute County?" Sunset had encountered a variety of killers in the wide-shouldered country but none who killed women. Then he went on, "But you said two months ago. You're sure late on the job."

"This Frank was right smooth," Charley explained. "In this boardin' house where the happy bride and groom were honeymoonin', the bride was found dead with a bullet in her head. There was a little pistol on the carpet beside her as though it had fallen from her hand. At first they figured it was suicide, although there wasn't a note. But when the happy husband didn't show up, the coroner got suspicious. The post-mortem brought the bullet out of the victim's head. It was a thirty-two calibre, same size as the pistol on the floor—"

"Yeah?"

"But the police found out that the slug from the bride's head didn't match those in the gun on the floor. So—the hunt was on for Frank."

"What makes you figure this Frank came up here?"

"About all we found at first was the record of a marriage licence. She was a Hilda Beddows of some little suburb around Boston. That was about all we did find."

"Snap it up, Charley."

"We took more interest after it was found she hadn't gunned herself over a busted romance. There was a fireplace in the room. Ashes in it like papers had been burnt." Charley drew a wallet from his inner coat pocket and opened it. "But part of the paper didn't burn. Maybe smoke blew it part way up the chimney. One of the officers found it stuck to the soot. That's why I came west."

Sunset smoothed out the sooty bit of paper and read the scrawling lines.

"Meet us in Buckskin, Frank—" That was all.

Sunset passed the bit of paper to Charley, who replaced it carefully in the wallet, then returned it to his pocket.

"Knowin' he had posed as a mining man, we made a list of Buckskins where there might be some mining excitement. It was my job to check 'em. Have you any idea at all how many Buckskins are scattered all over the West? I've been to Colorado, Arizona, New Mexico—"

"Always try Wyoming first, my boy."

"There are Buckskin canyons, Buckskin Bends, Buckskin this and Buckskin that. Why, a week ago I found a place named Buckskin River down in the Medicine Bow mountains. Then the sheriff tipped me off about a minin' excitement up north here at a camp called Buckskin. Known' this Frank dealt in mines, I tried my luck, I found it good—or bad—however you look at it, when everybody started shootin' and fightin' this mornin' and yellin', 'Buckskin or bust?'"

Sunset patted Charley on his fat shoulder. "We are so busy up here raisin' cattle and sheep, openin' up gold mines and the like, that we don't take time to think up nice original names for creeks and towns. Most of our creeks are called Dry or Sand or Cottonwood. Now you take in more civilised sections, they are really poetic about names. Like in New York they have the Waldorf Astoria Hotel. Now that's a dinger. Takes real thought. But out here most of our hotels are named after the folks who open the riffle—the Smith House or the Brown Hotel an' so forth. Or it's Bay Horse River or Cottonwood Mountain. Buckskin just happens to be located on the forks of a little old mountain creek named that. But I think you're on a hot trail, Charley. So we'll lope on into that camp and see if we can run down this Frank. What does he look like?"

Charley stood up and frowned. "That's one trouble. He's one of these nondescript fellows that aren't well remembered. Medium size. Ordinary clothing. But the landlady who rented the honeymoon room to Frank and Hilda remembered that he had brown eyes."

Sunset turned and looked toward Dulcy. She was walking Mildred up and down the road, soothing her. "The man who killed that drummer had brown eyes," he said. "But brown eyes are as common out here as cockleburs, I reckon." He shook his head. "What else you got besides that paper?"

Then Charley carefully drew a small parcel from his pocket, and revealed it was a pasteboard box. When he opened it, Sunset saw a snubby leaden slug nestling cosily in a wad of cotton.

"That," Charley said solemnly, "killed poor Hilda. It was found inside her head."

"No trace of relatives or friends of the victim?"

"Police are still hunting. But I left before they had really dug into the case. There was talk that this Hilda had a sister. It's been hard for me to connect with mail from home. But it would be nice for somebody if they were closely related to Hilda."

"How's that?"

"She had a bank account under her name of Beddows. There had been around twenty thousand in it. Lover boy got half, for they found the cheques. He had endorsed 'em. But she hadn't coughed up with the rest of it. So we thought—"

"You figured that's why he killed her, because she wouldn't give him all her money?"

Charley nodded. Then he asked, "What's our next move?"

"You seem to believe you were spotted by wearing a linen duster and posing as a salesman?"

"Yes. I was down around this Buckskin River, where Bill got DeBose. I was passing myself as a drummer there, wearing the duster and derby. They probably got word up here when I moved this way."

Sunset nodded. Then he said, "They'll soon discover that a mistake was made. So you must play dead for a bit."

"Play dead?"

"Yeah. Nobody but me, Bill, and the cook know you are the real detective. You go back to Jack's place and stay with Bill while we take the body to Buckskin and let on that the dead man is presumed to be Charley McBatt, a Boston dick."

Charley snorted. "Not much. Hang around with a wanted outlaw? Not me. Anyway, what good would all that faking do?"

Sunset smiled, recalling how Charley had resented his action in putting Bill on his honour not to quit the country. "We would be just playing a little poker with this gang in Buckskin," he explained. "Running a bluff so they might expose their hand. If they thought they had killed the man who was after Frank Flarity, they might not be so smart."

"How about this poor fellow who was killed?"

"I don't believe it'll take long, Charley. Not over

another day. He'll keep. Later on we can say a mistake was made and straighten things out."

Charley thought it over, then shrugged. There was a sour grin on his face. "It's your jurisdiction. If you think it will do any good, I'll try it. But, boy, it had better be good."

Sunset took out a notebook and pencil stub. He dashed off a note and handed it to Charley. "Word to Bill. Take my bay pony and head back. Help Bill hold the fort. If I need you, I'll send word by the Chinaman or somebody you can trust."

Charley went over and untied the bay pony. He regarded Sooner with a dubious eye. "I'm not much on horseback riding," he said. "Back in Boston—"

Sunset laughed. "Sit straight up and don't kick him in the ribs. And say—before you go—let me have that murder bullet from Boston. It's about the only clue in this case."

Reluctantly Charley turned over the pillbox containing the slug which had been extracted from the head of Hilda Beddows Flarity. Sunset put it in his pocket. "Don't lose it," Charley cautioned.

He climbed up on Sooner and, without thinking, kicked the bay in the ribs. Sooner looked around at Charley's feet, then bogged his head and threw the rider over his head into a bed of prickly pear cactus.

Dulcy and the others came up and watched Charley scramble painfully to his feet. "Where is he going?" the girl asked.

"Sight of blood sickens him to the stomach." said Sunset. "He's going back to Piute."

"That," Dulcy declared heartily, "should settle his stomach."

The horse had thrown its fat rider not far down

the road. Sunset hurried to help Charley. At first Charley swore he would not remount the jugheaded bay, which stood watching him with malevolent eyes. But Sunset assured him the little horse was gentle and willing to work.

"I told you not to kick him in the ribs. If you wore spurs that would be different—"

"How different?"

"Why, then he would have likely throwed you the length of the bridle reins. As it was, he just dumped you easy like fallin' out of bed."

"I tell you I won't ride him any more."

Sunset turned stern. "Then walk and lead him. But if you expect to overtake Wyoming miscreants, you had better learn to ride a pony."

Charley knew that if he went into Buckskin he stood a good chance of being murdered. The best play was to gain time in the search for Frank Flarity by running Sunset's dead man's bluff. Charley frowned, buttoned his coat tightly around his portly form and—assisted by the deputy—mounted. This time when Sooner, the bay, started down the road, Charley let the pony fix its own speed, which was very slow.

"But then," Sunset said, watching him, with Dulcy now at his side, "he's got all day."

"What do you mean? I thought he was sick and needed a doctor."

That startled Sunset. He turned and frowned down on the bright-eyed girl. "Well, I reckon," he explained slowly, "he would be in more pain ridin' fast than slow. When he gets to the road ranch, Bill can give him a drink of stomach bitters."

"Bill? Who is Bill?"

"Aw, that's the barkeeper."

"I heard somebody call him Jones."

This girl was a schoolmarm, therefore smart.

"I mind one who was too smart for her own good," Sunset reflected, and juggled the pillbox in his overalls pocket.

She said impatiently, "What are you mooning about? Everybody else called that barkeeper Jones. But you called him Bill."

"I know him better. He lets me use his first name. Bill Jones. Out here, only personal friends can use a man's first name."

She smiled and twinkled her eyes. "Well—what's your full name?"

"Full or sober, Miss Dulcy, they call me Sunset McGee." He removed his hat to exhibit his red hair. "Folks in Piute say that when I ride out of the west, looks like the sun going down." He waited expectantly but she didn't reveal her last name."

"They haven't called you Sunset all your life," she objected. "Your parents, for instance." She stared around at the rolling brown badlands. "I suppose you were born out here somewhere, along with the prairie dogs, Indians, and buffalo."

Sunset had to grin. "Stange to say," he explained, "few of us have been born out here. Me—I first saw daylight in Hoboken, New Jersey. My dad, a good old Irishman, worked on the docks before he got fed up, moved west, and took up a homestead down south in the plains. They're down there now. The old man runs a threshin' machine for the other grangers in the fall, tries to raise a crop rest of the year. My mother keeps him in line."

"She never called you Sunset."

He showed his white teeth in a grin. "No. I was first called Brian after an ancient king of Ireland. And you?" He was still hunting around. So she told him. She was Dulcy Pringle and she hailed from the west side of Chicago. Strangely enough, her father was a sergeant on the Chicago police force. But she had earned her own money for the past two years.

"Teaching school?"

She hesitated, frowned, bit her ripe red underlip. "That," she said slowly, "among other things."

"From the way you slung that coffee pot," Sunset said admiringly, "I reckon you put in some spare time pitching for a bloomer girls' baseball team."

Dulcy flushed. "Now," she burst out, "how did you ever guess? But it was sandlot stuff—just for fun."

They walked slowly to the coach. Jake and the Chinese had placed the dead man inside the vehicle. Milred sat forlornly by the road, her soft face streaked with tears. She dabbed at her eyes with a mite of a handkerchief as Dulcy walked up. "As soon as I can get a return ticket," she sobbed, "I am returning to Massachusetts."

Sunset stared at Mildred. Frank Flarity had come from Boston. The dead Hilda had taught school near that city. He started to ask the woman if she had known Hilda. But one question would lead to another. Better to hold back on investigating this eastern schoolmarm until the dead man in the coach had been revealed as Charles McBatt, Boston officer.

"Schoolmarms," growled Sunset, assisting Mildred and Dulcy into his buckboard, "are too darn smart."

Dulcy heard his muffled voice and asked sharply what he had said. But he answered that he was just telling Yum to get in and take care of Happy Jack.

Jake, the driver, after cutting the dead horse out of the traces, tied the other leader behind the coach. Then he headed slowly toward Buckskin with the wheel team labouring along, dragging the heavy Concord. Sunset followed with the buckboard. The two women crowded the seat. But Dulcy, for some strange reason, made Mildred sit in the middle.

CHAPTER VII

BUCKSKIN WAS WHAT THE WEST TERMED A roaring camp. The meat which caused it to roar was an unsolved problem. There were many such camps in the West. A few beef spreads in the hills hiring cowpunchers who blew in their wages, sheep outfits with herders just as free-handed, a mountain stream that plunged down from the high country carrying gold dust and nuggets which it deposited in the gravel banks along its course in the foothills. Some horny-handed grangers betting location money with the government that they wouldn't starve out before they proved up, jerkliners, tinhorns, prune merchants, railroad graders, town men.

"We have an estimated population of one thousand," drawled old man Smith, owner of the Smith House, main hotel. He was talking to Sunset as the two women registered for rooms. "Just how one thousand citizens can support ten saloons is beyond me. But we got ten saloons. And that's a fact."

"In Piute we hear the gold is pourin' in hand over fist."

Old man Smith sniffed. He had operated hotels in boom towns for the past twenty years, from Goldfield to Buckskin. "It's placer stuff on the crick up above the camp," he explained. "Some rich pockets have been found. As a result a crowd has stampeded in. They're the ones who are puttin' out gold hand over fist."

The coach with its dead burden and Sunset's rig had halted in front of the stage depot which was located near the hotel. Sunset had come in to assist the women in getting settled. It was a rough camp and they were far from home. Within five minutes it was apparent that Jake, the driver, had talked, and the grapevine had carried word all over town that two new women had arrived, both fairly good-looking.

The lobby began to fill up with a motley collection of males. Few were miners or graders, for the latter were hard at work at this hour, which was just before noon. But the riffraff of Buckskin, accustomed to feast its eyes only on painted dance hall entertainers, had taken time off for a look at the two schoolmarms.

These Buckskinners were bold only of eye. At that time in the untamed West, a decent woman could travel wherever she desired without being molested. Dulcy flushed a little, but met the men's scrutiny with a toss of her blonde head and a glint in her blue eyes. Mildred demurely signed the register, the red bird on her hat bobbing as she bent over the desk.

Behind this desk stood old Smith's clerk. He had apparently just come on duty, for he was freshly shaven and dressed in neat dark garments and spotless white shirt. His dark silk tie was thrust through a small gold ring. The clerk was slender, quick-moving, and wore a small sandy brown moustache beneath his small pert nose. As the light was bad due to the lamp over the desk, he wore a green shade to protect his eyes. In the manner of most clerks in hotels, he read the guests' signatures as they wrote in the book, reading upside down as a printer does.

The clerk called to the proprietor in a bright chirpy voice, "Mister Smith, here's one of your relatives from Massachusetts."

Old Smith turned and frowned. He wore a massive white beard that reached to his middle shirt button. He was bald-headed and chewed tobacco. He looked for a spittoon before he answered. "None of my folks in the East," he drawled.

The clerk laughed. "I was just joshing," he admitted. "Meet Miss Mildred Smith from Boston. Here to teach school along with Miss Dulcy Pringle from Chicago."

Mildred beamed and twittered while Dulcy almost made old Smith swallow his cud with one of her flashing smiles. The entire lobby laughed at the clerk's joke. One tinhorn chuckled and piped up, "There are probably a hundred Smiths in this camp."

"And just as many Joneses," said another.

Sunset swung around and said solemnly. "Now is the time for all good Smiths and true to come to the aid of the party."

Some of his listeners recognised Sunset as the Piute law. "What you oratin' about now?" he was asked.

"This," said Sunset. "Jack Coogan, well and favourably known to plenty of you, was roughed up this morning by Buckskin toughs, allegedly over your comin' town election. They were led by a red-muzzled hombre named One-Eared Budge. Jack's been carried in to Doc Backhammer for treatment. We don't know whether he will live or die. So what I meant was this. Now is the time for all good men and true—"

Three men came into the lobby, ploughing their way through the staring crowd. Men didn't wish to give way, but they pushed ahead arrogantly. The three were led by the lanky man Sunset had fought with in the road ranch bar and later had identified as Slim Osage, wanted in Sweetwater County for murder.

Any mishaps Slim had suffered in the fight had apparently been overcome. He staggered as he approached the desk and regarded the deputy with whisky-shot, hostile eyes.

"The law," stated Slim Osage, halting his two henchmen a dozen feet from where Sunset stood with back to the desk, "is supposed to be impartial in elections. You are a limb of the law. Therefore," Slim tilted his twisted blue nose in contempt, "in solicitin' votes, you are away out of line."

Sunset heard the hotel owner speak swiftly to the women: "Step around here back of the desk," and knew that they would be barricaded behind that heavy piece of furniture. So Sunset braced himself for a showdown with Slim and his mates. They had been oiling up at one of the ten saloons. He could smell the whisky reek where he stood. In this country a man shouldn't start getting drunk before dusk. He might wind up with a powerful headache caused by a forty-five slug inside his skull.

"Mister Osage," Sunset drawled, "your remarks are well chosen. The law is impartial. But you will recollect that I merely encouraged decent citizens to cast votes. I didn't mention any candidates."

Osage had a snaky head and a long skinny neck. He jerked his head down between his shoulders and slitted his eyes until only a red dangerous glitter could be seen. He wore a long gun, and he had jerked it around so that it hung within easy reach. One of his mates resembled another member of the gang who had engaged Sunset at the road ranch, but the deputy could not be sure. However, in this game, Slim Osage was the answer. Whatever happened to Slim would decide what would come next.

"You have miscalled me," Slim stated flatly. "My name's not Slim Osage. My name is Bill Smith and I'm a miner."

Sunset answered just as flatly. "You are wanted for horse theft in Sweetwater County and there's five hundred dollars on you under the name of Slim Osage. You are under arrest as of now."

Slim laughed boldly and turned his head to grin at the crowd. Some had cheered when he gave his name as Smith. There he made his mistake. Before he could regain his watchful pose, Sunset was upon him. Swiftly, as a falcon dropping upon its quarry, he crossed the intervening space in three long jumps. He was all over Slim Osage before the latter could clear a gun. Sunset's left fist snapped off Slim's twisted nose. Slim wobbled, tried to fight. Sunset dropped his right hand. He had used it to whip a set of steel cuffs from his belt as he made his attack. He snapped down one cuff and it clicked around Slim's right wrist. Sunset gave it a painful wrench which made Slim yelp.

"Drop your gun," said Sunset, "or I'll tear your hand off your arm."

Slim's gun clanged on the floor. Sunset put his boot on it. He jerked his prisoner to him and held him there. He looked over Slim's writhing shoulder at Slim's open-mouthed warriors.

"If you aim to start shootin'," said Sunset, "you'll have to drive your lead through Slim to hit me."

He saw that neither of the two would dare a shoot-out, but also that they were men not easily bluffed. Slim Osage struggled, but the cuff cut cruelly into his flesh. His breath was hot against Sunset's face, and the

horse thief was cursing and calling down maledictions
upon the red head of his captor.

Sunset felt a momentary twinge because he had
jumped Slim Osage in front of two good women and
thus caused Slim to spout foul language. On account
of the women, the deputy had refrained from making
a gun play. Slim's artillery had not worried him, but
a wild bullet might possibly down Dulcy or Mildred.
Schoolmarms were smart, but one of them might get
hysterical and duck out from behind the desk. Sunset
managed to lock the other cuff on Osage's left wrist
before the two henchmen closed with him. With both
hands he shoved Slim toward them. One man paused
briefly to grab Slim before the latter fell flat on the
floor. The other, dodging past, came in on Sunset
with fists flying.

Sunset reeled from a Sunday punch that landed on
his jaw. This blow whistled in before he could put
up his guard after cuffing Slim Osage. As he rocked
back and forth on his boots, shaking his head to clear
away the fog, his attacker hit a second time and
knocked Sunset off his feet. He went down on his
knees. He felt suddenly sick and dizzy. But he reached
out and closed his arms in a football tackle around
his attacker's legs. He tightened his grip. The man
yelled and plunged over on his back, with Sunset
following him to the floor. They sprawled there a
moment in panting silence. Sunset was fighting to get
back his senses. Those two punches had half stunned
him.

He was flattened out on top of the heaving frame
of the man who had hit him. He could look down
into the fellow's bloodshot eyes. And even in this
extremity, Sunset thought hazily to himself that the

eyes he saw were a glary grey like the eyes of a trapped wolf.

At this moment the man who had grabbed Slim let his boss drop to the floor with a thud. He came to his mate's rescue as the latter choked out a yell for help.

"I'm comin', Dob!" he shouted hoarsely. "Hang on!"

That war cry cleared Sunset's brain of battle fog. He knew well enough that he'd be a target as long as he lay humped over the body of the man on the floor. It was time to change partners, as they said in a quadrille.

With a mighty kick to the side, Sunset rolled over, carrying with him the body of the man he had held down. He hung desperately to the latter as he made the turn, for as he rolled his eye caught the flash of a descending gun barrel. If Sunset had remained atop his man, the gun steel would have cracked down on the top of his red pate. As it was, the steel thudded down and brought a yell from the fellow named Dob. Dob wheezed out in agony, "Hold 'er, Sam! You about busted my shoulder!"

But Sam, disregarding his mate's shout, dropped to a knee to take better aim with his gun barrel at Sunset's head. Sunset kicked out like a horse and cut one of Sam's legs from under him. Sam came down on Sunset and Dob like a sack of flour. As Sunset was now on the bottom of the pile, this sudden increase in weight drove all the wind from his body.

But Dob had also suffered from the fall of Sam. And the latter, unbalanced, was briefly out of the fight. All three battlers had reached the point where they required lots of fresh air. As for Slim Osage, since being handcuffed, he had not come to the aid of his two henchmen.

Sunset knew that now he was in a tight corner. He lay almost flat on his back on the floor. He had flung both his arms around Dob and held the latter to him, face down, in a tight embrace. Every time Dob gulped for air, he was so near that he robbed Sunset of western atmosphere. As for Sam, he had tripped and fallen and now lay arched over Dob's back.

Even as his heart hammered against his ribs and his lungs fought frenziedly for fresh air on the dusty hotel floor, Sunset was striving to force his numbed mind to come back into full-scale operation. His head felt dead from the neck up but he had to think his way out of this one. Otherwise Sam would rise up, get in a lucky brain-cracking blow, and wind up the course of true law right under the eyes of Dulcy. That could not be allowed.

Sunset gambled that Dob would not have wind or strength enough for a good hearty punch. He held to the man with his right arm but he dropped his left. He shot up his left hand and took Dob by his corded throat. He dug his thumb into Dob's neck just below the ear. He began to strangle Dob. Dob kicked and writhed like a spring chicken just beheaded. But Sunset hung grimly, tightening his choking hold on Dob's throat. The man's face turned black. His eyes popped and his tongue protruded. Now and then he raised an agonised squawk.

Big Sam arose. He was dazed from his fall. He stepped back a pace to decide on his next move. This gave Sunset a split second in which to edge out from beneath Dob's crushing weight. Dob continued to kick and jerk, but aimlessly. If Sunset maintained his present grip, Dob would die as surely as if he had been dropped from a hangman's gallows.

Sunset's gun was trapped beneath him, but now the fingers of his right hand, still tight around the body of Dob, touched the cold stock of the latter's gun where it had been hiked up by the fury of the fight. Sunset chanced another big risk. If the weapon hung up in a tight holster, then Sam would move in before he could jerk out Dob's gun. Sam and Dob were bullies and gunfighters. Sunset decided they would not wear their guns too tightly encased in holsters. Grabbing the hilt of Dob's gun, he made a swift draw.

Sam, stepping in for further battle, suddenly found himself staring down into the tilted barrel of his friend's gun. And still under the frame of Dob, Sam also saw the wild red hair and the blazing eyes of Sunset McGee. McGee, bloody and battered, spit bloody froth as he snarled, "Stay clear or I kill you!"

Sam remained a moment, undecided. Thereby he lost his chance to win. He should have dared Sunset and killed the deputy as he lay on the floor. Quite likely Sam was in a better position for the shootout. All Sam lacked was the last ultimate inch of cold nerve.

Dob was out of this fight. His kicks and lunges had weakened. He was in fact at the point of death. Sunset removed his fingers from where they had gouged into Dob's throat. Dob rolled weakly off the deputy and lay gasping on the floor like a big trout fresh from the creek. There were deep red gouges, the prints of Sunset's fingers, four on one side of Dob's neck, the thumb print on the other. Sunset felt weak too. But when Dob rolled off, he hoisted himself with his left hand into sitting position. His right trained Dob's gun on Sam. The latter stood tensely watchful.

Sunset spoke again, now quite forgetful of the ladies present. "Damn you," he snarled. "Either use your gun or throw it away."

Sam licked his lips. He waited. Then suddenly he attempted to get back into the war. He raised his right arm for a snap shot at the bloody man sitting on the floor. Sunset fired. He put his bullet through Sam's right forearm, turning it into a bloody wreck. The kick of a forty-five slug rivals that of a mule. Sam came down with a crash on his knees. He howled, knelt there holding his blasted right arm while blood gushed from it.

Sunset staggered to his boots. He was weak as a cat. He eyed Sam, then turned his blurred gaze on Dob. There were fifty men in the lobby now, but they were silent as a congregation in church. The air was rank with the smell of burnt gunpowder, men's blood and sweat. Sunset said heavily to the men nearest him, "Fetch Doc Backhammer!" Then he turned and looked for cuffed Slim Osage.

A man said to him, "Slim never waited. He ducked out the back door with the cuffs on."

Sunset listened, nodded; then, half reeling, he lurched across the open space where he had fought. He braced his shoulders against the desk to prevent himself from collapsing.

CHAPTER VIII

AT THAT MOMENT, WHEN SUNSET BELIEVED he would surely fall flat on his face, a loud metallic clangour rang out in the lobby. At first it reminded Sunset of the volunteer firemen of Piute making a run to a blaze. Somehow the vibrant ear-splitting noise cleared his wits. Shaking his head, he half-turned and saw that double doors at the far end of the lobby had been pushed open. A Chink cook stood there holding an iron triangle, banging out a loud refrain upon it, calling Buckskinners to the noon meal in old Smith's grub emporium.

What amazed the sore-faced Sunset was that the cook was his friend, Yum, who had arrived in town with him a scant half-hour before. Good cooks were a scarce article in the desert hills. The thrifty Yum had perhaps found old Smith's kitchen force shorthanded and picked up a job right away.

There was a beatific smile on Yum's moon face as he rang the triangle. Apparently his stomach pains had faded away. The thought flashed through Sunset's mind that perhaps Yum had located one of Charley's bottles of Pain Killer.

Two bloody battered men sprawled on the floor. Fifty others ringed them. But the moment the triangle rang out, the entire crowd headed for the dining room, each man pushing and fighting to get in the lead. They reminded Sunset of a herd of starving dogie steers being turned in for the first time to a hay yard. His mouth hurt but he had to curl his lower lip at the cold indifference to suffering shown by the men of this camp. Fifty of them, but not a man jack to wait and try to staunch the blood flowing from Sam's arm or help Dob regain his wind. Of course, the two deserved little pity. Yet they were suffering humans.

That indifference of the ragtag of Buckskin revealed more clearly than words to the deputy why a gang had taken control of the town. The Buckskinners thought only of themselves, their chance to get rich quickly. This was a mass exhibition of calloused selfishness. That was why a good man like Jack Coogan had been hazed out of town and beaten to the point of death when he tried to speak up for law and order and ordinary decency.

But what about old man Smith and his chipper hotel clerk? Sunset circled slowly, clinging to the desk for support. His legs felt wobbly below the knees. His eyes, too, were misted over with salty sweat. When he licked his lips, he tasted blood.

When he had turned his head, he found himself staring into the double barrels of a sawed-off shotgun. The weapon was held by the hotel clerk. Old man Smith stood at the far end of the desk with his hands resting upon it. There was a pained look in the hotel keeper's eyes, a sick look on his face as though he had just swallowed his cud of tobacco.

The sight of the shotgun—both barrels cocked too as Sunset immediately noted—amazed the deputy. He had not expected the neatly attired clerk to step into this fight.

Sunset was thankful for one thing at least. The two women were not in sight. They were, perhaps, still hiding below the top of the desk.

"What ails you?" Sunset asked the clerk.

"This here is a family hotel," the clerk replied briskly. "A fight like you just staged is apt to drive away trade. And, to boot, you have caused that Sam to bleed all over our floor."

Amazed, Sunset looked from the hostile clerk to Smith. But the old man remained stubbornly silent. Sunset had heard Smith was a tough but straight man not easily bluffed. But here this dandified clerk had taken over the old man's hotel, lock, stock, and shotgun barrels.

"I didn't aim to stage a fight," Sunset explained carefully to the clerk. "I'm the law. I hold papers showing Slim Osage is wanted for murder. When I put him under arrest, this Dob and Sam jumped me. It wasn't really a fight—"

The clerk smiled thinly. "It was more like a riot," he drawled. "Well, if you are the law, produce the papers on Slim."

Sunset fumbled in one breast pocket of his shirt. Then, just as suddenly, he recalled that he had not put the wanted notice on Slim there when he revealed his travelling library to Boston Charley at the road ranch. No, he had put it with the other folders in a saddle pocket on his bay. And he had allowed Charley to ride the pony back to the road ranch without first retrieving his folders on men wanted whom he hoped to find in Buckskin.

But Slim was cuffed up and would wait. This was but a passing breeze of the gathering storm. Sunset sought to grin amiably upon the clerk but his face hurt. All he could do was grimace like a man with an ulcerated wisdom tooth. He dug into his vest pocket which, strangely enough, had not been torn off in the fight. From it he produced the small silver badge which denoted authority granted by the sheriff of Piute. He laid it on top of the open hotel register. The clerk deigned to glance briefly at the shining emblem. Then he raised the eyes under the green shade and sniffed so that his breath gently ruffled the scanty brown moustache that grew above his tight mouth.

"Those three men," the clerk declared, "are registered here as our guests. They have paid in advance for a week. Since you are the law, you'll admit that you are away out of line. A man can't be taken out of his home without first being confronted with a warrant."

Sunset opened his eyes wide in honest admiration. "Every time I turn around since I first hit this Buckskin range," he acknowledged, "I am confronted with a vast knowledge of the law. There was Mister Osage oratin' and spoutin' before he felt the steel cuffs. And Mister Dob and Mister Sam, his friends, springin' to his aid in the sacred name of Liberty, Equality, and all the rest." Sunset shook his head, watching the clerk and the gun, wondering what colour were the eyes under the green shade. Then his voice sharpened. "Whatever your name is, friend, quit joshin'. Put up that gun and quit interferin' with me."

"You have caused a riot in my place of business," the clerk retorted in his chipper voice that grated on Sunset's nerves like a saw being filed.

"And I'm right apt to start another," snapped Sunset. Then, as he caught the implication of the clerk's statement, he looked at old Smith. "I thought you owned this dump," he said.

Before the old man could reply, the clerk cut in,

"Don't call it a dump. Only first-class joint in town."

"Joint then; excuse me."

"I have just taken over a working interest in this hotel. Mr. Smith will tell you that I have become his partner within the past twenty-four hours." The clerk cast a sharp glance at Smith. "Tell him that, you old goat."

Old Smith gagged on his cud. His face had turned almost as white as his long saintly beard. He looked into Sunset's face, and now the deputy saw the old man's dim eyes clearly. Sunset read entreaty, dumb desperation, utter fear in their hazy depths.

"You—you are not—" the old man croaked. Then he checked and licked his lips.

"Take your time," the clerk encouraged. "Tell this hayseed deputy all about our business deal, Smith. How you felt that you were getting too old to run a hotel in a wild camp. You needed a younger, more alert man for partner. So you made a deal with me."

Smith glanced from Sunset to the shotgun with cocked barrels; then again he raised sick eyes. "I made a deal with you," he whispered.

Sunset saw that there was something deadly wrong here. They had previously run a good man like Jack Coogan out of Buckskin. Had this old man's turn come? It appeared to be the case.

Sunset said gently to the clerk but there was a steel foundation to his drawling voice, "You'll have to change the name of this hotel, I reckon. Now it is the Smith House—"

The clerk twisted his thin lips into one of his peculiar chilly smiles. "From now on it will be advertised far and near as the Firebank Hotel. Lodgings of the best quality to be found for man and beast."

Sunset stepped back from the desk. Again he was amazed. So here stood the pet of the tough gang. Fred Firebank. What did they call this neat clerk with the deadly grin? Fearless Freddy. Even Big Freddy. But he was not a large man, just a medium-sized fellow. He was well dressed for a rough camp, but he'd blend into a crowd anywhere. Nothing obtrusive about Fearless Fred with the exception of his cocked sawed-off shotgun. So Fred had taken over the main hotel in Buckskin.

Sunset tried to bow mockingly but found that his neck hurt from the various punches that had been landed in the fight. "We must find time," he cooed to Freddy, "to get better acquainted. Right now—I came in here to see that the two ladies got good rooms."

"The two ladies," Fred Firebank snapped, "are being taken care of."

Sunset stretched out his long neck. He hoped to look over the top of the desk and see Dulcy and Mildred cowering on the floor. The clerk went on coldly, "I told you that we protect our guests from roughnecks. While you were battling around, throwing wild bullets, I saw that the two women were properly escorted to their rooms on the second floor."

"In that case, Freddy, I'd like the room numbers. I'll step up and assure myself they are comfortable."

"Don't call me Freddy. They are comfortable. You have your orders to *step*. Right out of this hotel."

"All your friends call you Freddy? Fellows like Slim and One-Eared Budge."

"Only my friends call me Freddy. To you, I am *Mister* Fred Firebank."

"Very well, Mister Fred Firebank. And now, if you'll quit funnin' around with that darned scatter gun, I'll step up and see how those ladies are gettin' by. That Mildred from Massachusetts is a right timid soul at times."

"I tell you those women are being taken care of. Now, get out before I lose my temper." Firebank tilted the gun. "You have no legal right here. You've been warned—"

"Be careful of that cannon, Freddy—"

"Don't call me Freddy."

"That cannon might go off accidental and knock down some of your lobby decorations."

"If it goes off," Fred said grimly, "it will knock a hole in you big enough to hold a hive of bees."

"I forgot and left my badge there on the desk." Sunset said plaintively.

Freddy muttered to Old Smith, "Pick up the badge and give it to him—*hard*."

The old man reached out and seized the law's emblem. Prodded by fear, he threw it at Sunset's toes. It gleamed there on the floor in dust and blood. It was a calculated insult. Sunset's gorge arose. He gripped a six-gun. This was close quarters to go against a man armed with a shotgun and barricaded behind a desk. Then the red surge of anger receded. Sunset recalled that his Piute boss had advised him to exercise tact and diplomacy in Buckskin. There had been a mention of the county expense of pauper burials. Taxpayers were apt to object to such items when the old sheriff again ran for office.

Sunset bent to pick up the badge. As he half-knelt, Fearless Freddy offered the final insult. Leaning over the top of the desk, he spat upon the badge. Sunset looked up into Freddy's grinning face, the pursed lips. In insulting the emblem of the law, Freddy had forgotten his usual caution. His body, slanting over the desk, was now resting upon the shotgun.

Moved by a powerful burst of rage which he could not overcome, Sunset whipped back the six-gun he held—the gun he had taken from Dob. He hurled it straight into the face of Freddy. Freddy dodged the shining projectile as it whizzed toward his face. The gun narrowly missed him. Sailing past his head, it changed against the hotel keyboard.

Both barrels of the shotgun roared smoke and slugs. If Sunset had been upright, the charges would have ploughed into his brisket. But he was on his knees. The buckshot whisked over his bobbing head. Then the deputy, lunging to his feet, sought to climb over the desk and come to grips with Fred Firebank. But the clerk whirled and scuttled around the end of the desk. He struck the lowest step of the flight of stairs that led to the hotel's second floor. Sunset, seeing that his lunge had been a vain one, plopped his boots back on the lobby floor. In turn, he angled around the desk, body arched out, both arms extended in an effort to tackle Firebank.

Sunset had eyes only for the flying form of Firebank. He did not see the white-coated figure that came dodging in from the flank with an extended leg. Sunset fell over the leg. He crashed to the floor. He lay there, propping himself up on his arms, staring up the stairway. Firebank stood on the top step, staring down with a triumphant smile on his face. Then Firebank shouted shrilly, "Good work, Chink!" and with a flirt of his neat coat tails, he turned and darted out of sight.

Sunset straightened up and stared, amazed, into the placid face of the man who had tripped him. The man in the white coat who had come running to Firebank's aid was Yum, of all men! Yum, the faithful, cook, from Coogan's place. In Buckskin, it seemed, faith and loyalty and friendship counted for nothing.

Sunset shook his head sadly. All his wrath had faded away. "You," he choked out, with a vast regret. "Of all men—*you*. The friend of Happy Jack!"

Yum continued to regard Sunset without losing his wide grin. "Me workee now all same Mister Firebank. Better you get out."

"But Jack Coogan?"

"You no hear yet? Jack, *he* die."

Sunset sprang to his feet, the weariness of battle forgotten. He tried to grab Yum by his white coat. The cook nimbly evaded him. And at the same time, Yum produced a slim carving knife.

"When did Jack die? We took him to Doc Backhammer," Sunset cried out.

"Jack die while you fightee. So no more bossee man for me." Yum shrugged. "My cousin, he work here, all same kitchen. Right away quick Mister Flirebank give me good job helpin' him."

Men such as Firebank were doing strange things to the original settlers of Buckskin—taking over hotels from men like Smith; winning the loyalty of the formerly faithful like Yum. What was it? The urge to get rich quick, inspired by the coarse yellow gold brought into Buckskin?

Sunset stared curiously into Yum's bland face. "You sure look plumb satisfied with yourself," he drawled. "Don't even need any more Painkiller for your stomach."

"Make big money now. Buy all Painkiller I need."

Sunset turned on his heel. He saw that Sam and

Dob had vanished. A trail of blood led to the doorway. Well, they had friends up the street in the dives and deadfalls. Sunset turned back to the foot of the stairway. Yum still held position there, the light glittering coldly on his knife bladd.

"Get out of my way," Sunset commanded sharply. "And don't make any false moves with that toad stabber."

He carried his own gun in his holster. He wondered briefly if he'd be forced to gun this Chink who had, until lately, been his friend. But Yum grinned and stepped aside. "You go now," he agreed. "Find lady okay."

Sunset took his time climbing the steps. Fred Firebank might be waiting at the top with a ready gun. But no burst of gunfire disputed his arrival on the second floor. Sunset paused a moment, surveying the long gloomy hall with the closed doors of rooms opening off it. At the far end an oblong of light indicated an outside doorway. Toward this Sunset made his way.

He proceeded alertly. Firebank might at any moment step from one of the rooms and open fire. Marksmanship would be difficult in this gloomy hallway. Sunset wished that he had discovered the number of the room taken by the two women. That would have shortened his worry and his risk. He wanted to assure himself that Dulcy and Mildred were safe, then hasten down to consult with Doc Backhammer about the death of Happy Jack Coogan.

As he passed a door midway of the hall, a muffled drumming came to his ears. He paused, then saw that the key was in the lock. He put his head to an upper panel. Again the dull drumming began. It halted for a moment, and in that interval Sunset grinned wryly at sound of some choice cuss words spoken in a girlish voice. Dulcy was locked inside the room. She had kicked vainly to open the locked door. Before she could wear out her slipper toes, Sunset called in a low voice, "What'll you give me if I unlock this door?"

At first the girl didn't recognise his voice. "Open it!" she cried out sharply, "or I'll kick it open!"

"I'll open up for you, Miss Dulcy. But hold your kicks as I walk in."

Unlocking the door, he opened it cautiously. He remembered the Chicago girl's skill as a pitcher. She might throw a slipper at his head. She awaited him in the doorway, holding a chair in her hands as though to repel attack. On beyond her, Sunset glimpsed Mildred, and her red bird hat, half collapsed on an iron bedstead.

When Dulcy recognised the grinning features of the deputy, she flushed and carefully set the chair legs on the floor. "Another second," she breathed, "and I would have caved in your handsome skull."

"May I come in?" he asked.

She smiled, indicated the recumbent Mildred. "We're well chaperoned. Come ahead."

CHAPTER IX

Quickly she explained how it happened that she was here with Mildred in this locked room. While Sunset's whole attention was centred on his fight, one of Firebank's men had come down the stairway, undoubtedly called by Freddy's bell. She hadn't wanted to go up the stairs. But the man had held a gun and frightened Mildred. Dulcy had accompanied the older woman so that she would not faint from terror. The guard had offered no rudeness. He had ushered them into this room, then locked the door.

"He left the key outside," observed Sunset.

"That's strange," said Dulcy.

"Not so strange. Maybe Freddy told him to leave it there so he could come up later for a little visit."

"But he'd have a pass key to all the locks, wouldn't he?"

"Might have mislaid it. The Smith House is all upset today. New management. Even got a new cook." And Sunset mentioned Yum.

That infuriated Dulcy. "To think he'd throw in with the gang that hurts his boss."

"You mean—*killed* his boss. Happy Jack just died down at Doc Backhammer's."

Mildred, now resting on the bed with her tearful face buried in a limp pillow, heard the news of Jack's death. She raised up with a little shriek. Her eyes were big and wet and round. She sat on the edge of the bed and gazed pitifully at Dulcy. The latter had seated herself on a small stool near the dressing table and politely offered the room's best chair, a wickerwork rocker, to Sunset.

"Dulcy!" Mildred half screamed. "Let's go home! Forget why we ever came out to this heathenish country!"

Dulcy stood up and walked gracefully over to Mildred. She bent and put her arm around the weeping woman, soothing her as though she were a child. Mildred, in her hysterical fear, had forgotten to remove the hat with the red bird on it. Sunset, watching, saw the bright feathers bob and flirt around as though the bird were alive and trying to escape from the hat. This was an illusion created by the nervous twitchings of Mildred's head as it rested against one of Dulcy's staunch shoulders.

"I want to go home," Mildred wailed. "I should never have come here."

Sunset was about to add his two bits worth and say that education would suffer. But then Dulcy said a strange thing to Mildred. "You're the boss," Dulcy drawled in her easy manner. "You hired me to come with you. It's up to you—"

Sunset stood up, frowning. "But you are schoolmarms," he said. "The town will do the hiring."

Dulcy stared back at the deputy. Then she whispered, "Somebody may be listening to us. See what became of Firebank."

Sunset stepped into the hall. Nobody was in sight. He slipped cautiously down the hallway, seeking to discover if any of the rooms were now occupied. But the second floor was silent as the grave. He came at last to the doorway at the end of the hall, peered out and saw that an iron stairway led down to the alley in the rear of the hotel. He decided that Firebank had escaped down this stairway. He came back to Dulcy's room, re-entered, carefully closed and locked the door. Then he faced her.

"If you keep your voice down," he said reassuringly, "I don't believe you'll be heard."

Dulcy seated herself on the edge of the bed. Mildred was resting again with her head on the pillow, but she hadn't taken off her hat. The red bird fascinated Sunset.

"First," Dulcy half whispered, "I must be sure I dare talk to you. We are two lone women—"

He produced the badge which Fred Firebank had lately insulted. With a grim smile on his face, he revealed it to the girl. "Bring it nearer," she said. "I can't read what's engraved on it from where I'm sitting."

He stepped over and held the gleaming badge on his palm while she bent her blonde head and closely examined the inscription on it which informed the world that the wearer was a deputy sheriff of Piute County. Then Dulcy raised her face, arched her black brows, and looked up into Sunset's battered face with a faint smile on her full lips. She stared for what seemed hours to Sunset; then suddenly she revealed her white teeth in an open smile. She laughed.

"I had to bet on my knowledge of frank and honest faces," she explained, "so I could trust you. Any crook could be carrying a badge like this. Well," she lowered her voice to a whisper, "I am not here to hunt a job teaching school. I came West to find a man."

Sunset gulped and reddened. "You mean you're one of these heart and hand girls, hunting for a husband? One of these girls who advertise and the like?"

Dulcy laughed again, a friendly laugh that reminded Sunset of a silver bell. She explained again, "I came West to find a man, but not for *love*. The man I'm hunting is a cold murderer. And his name is Frank Flarity."

This was too much for Sunset. This pretty girl sought the same human beast as did Boston Charley. Were the two working together? But Charley had not mentioned that the girl knew of his pursuit of the wife killer. Sunset walked back and sat down on the rocking chair.

"I reckon, lady," he said slowly, "we got to talk." He glanced around, wondering if these thin walls had ears. "And keep your voice away down low."

"You understand," she whispered, "why I said I had to bet on you being what you claimed: an honest man of the law." She bent swiftly, whipped up the hem of her long skirt. She wore high button shoes. From the top of the right shoe she plucked a tiny golden object. She held it out in her palm toward the dazzled eyes of Sunset. It was a little golden badge, similar in shape to Sunset's emblem.

"Do you understand what it is?" she asked.

He nodded.

"As I told you before," Dulcy went on, "I am the daughter of a Chicago police officer. I did teach school for a year. But the work proved uninteresting. So I went to work for a large department store as a detective. The work was mostly concerned with catching store thieves, what we call shoplifters."

"I've heard of 'em," nodded Sunset. His eyes were popping. So here sat a lady John Law. Well, Chicago could show old Wyoming a thing or two. And maybe Buckskin.

Dulcy hurried on. Her experienced father had given her plenty of help and advice. She had advanced in her profession until she found herself called on now and then for special assignments.

"But I never before was mixed up in a murder," said

Dulcy, "until my little friend, Mildred, came to me for help."

She had met Mildred during the year she had taught school. Mildred was really from Massachusetts but she had come West to teach in the Chicago schools. "I thought she was all alone in the world then," said Dulcy. "She was such a sweet thing that we became firm friends. We wrote back and forth when I went to work for the store and she returned to her home in the East. Then—a few weeks ago—Mildred wrote and asked me to help her. I have the letter along with other written credentials."

"Mildred," she whispered, "asked my help. She said that her sister had been murdered by the husband, a man she called Frank Flarity. So—"

Before she could go on, the door quivered to a thunderous assault upon it from the other side—banging and kicking as though a battering ram was being used. Then a voice, ringing with anger shouted. "Open up or I'll shoot out the lock!"

Sunset leaped from his chair. He cried to Dulcy, "Help me with Mildred! Get down on the floor! Might be some of Firebank's bunch!"

Mildred screamed as they seized her. Dulcy smothered her shriek by putting her hand over Mildred's mouth. Dulcy pinned her hysterical friend to the floor. Crouching there, she watched Sunset unlatch his gun, then approach the door.

"One more kick on this door," Sunset warned, "and I'll start pumpin' lead through it!"

The battering ended abruptly. Then came the harsh reply: "So it's the Piute law, hey. Well—*open up!* This is Lonesome Luke."

"What do you want?"

"To make sure them ladies are safe."

Sunset grinned over his shoulder at the wide-eyed Dulcy. He nodded toward the writhing form of Mildred. "Luke means your friend," he drawled. He turned the key, stepped aside, and waited alertly.

The lean grey man entered almost on the lope, like a lobo wolf. He carried a gun. His bleak chilly glare swept Sunset, then came to rest on the women. Dulcy smiled up into Luke's bony face.

"She's safe, Mister Luke," said Dulcy.

Luke relaxed. He sighed gustily. "She better be safe," he announced. He lowered his gun carefully. He repeated, turning his cold eyes on Sunset, "You *bet* she better be safe. What's your business in here with 'em? Door locked and so on. And her sobbin' that way."

Dulcy took her hand away from Mildred's mouth. She stood up swaying, straightened her clothing, then bent to assist her friend. But before she could take Mildred's imploring hands, Lonesome Luke intervened. With two long strides, he crossed the room, bent, swooped up Mildred. He stood as though lost to the world. And—strangely—Mildred crept thankfully into his embrace. She buried her wet face against his shoulder, and wept as though her heart had just been broken. The red bird on her hat bobbed erractically as Luke raised his gun hand—for he had slid his pistol into his belt—and awkwardly patted Mildred on her head.

"There, there," Luke crooned. "Hang to old Luke. Nobody's goin' to hurt you none in this camp, nor anywhere else. You just hang to old Luke and cry your eyes out."

Stepping away, Dulcy laid a finger on her lips to hide a smile. She came over to Sunset. "It looks to me," she whispered, "like love at first sight."

Sunset shook his head. "Mildred from Massachusetts," he agreed, "may seem a little soft. But she has sure busted down the toughest proposition in Wyoming. She has made Lonesome Luke into a besotted slave."

"Don't you believe in love at first sight?" the girl asked.

She was standing so near that he was again aware of her warm beauty. She wasn't the weeping type. She wasn't giving him an excuse to embrace her. It was strange how a hard-case hombre like Lonesome Luke would go for a little thing like Mildred.

"Love," said Dulcy as though reading his thoughts, "is always to be wondered at. It is never understood. The strangest things always happen."

She was teasing him. Her breath felt soft upon his cheek. Sunset swung around. Before she could resist, he took her in his arms. She resisted. Then—as his lips sought her smooth cheek—she relaxed a moment, but only a moment. The kiss was long, sweet. It thrilled Sunset to his toes. Then Dulcy broke from him. She faced him, flushed, with flashing eyes. She drew back her hand as though to strike him. The black brows arched stormily. She considered his stubborn but amazed face, then shrugged and laughed, "Well," she said, "I suppose I really invited that. But I didn't come West to be kissed."

He didn't believe she was an arrant flirt. A man could find plenty of girls in Buckskin whose kisses could be bought for a drink of whisky. He wanted to explain just why he had taken her in his arms, why he had kissed her. He couldn't quite find the words. He should have known better. She wasn't that sort of a girl, an easy mark.

"Forget it," she cut in sharply. "There's more important work here for us."

"More important?" he rapped out.

She gestured toward Mildred crying in the arms of Luke. "She must stay with her bargain, never go home until she has helped me to find the man who murdered her sister. Never until we overtake Frank Flarity."

Mildred tugged to free herself from Luke. The lean man stood glowering. He raised his hand, laid it on the hilt of his gun.

"Dulcy," Mildred cried wildly, "don't mention that name! Don't speak it, ever again. He might be near—try to kill me—"

"Frank Flarity," Dulcy began, facing Mildred, turning her back to the doorway.

Sunset also stood with his back to the doorway. His eyes were upon Lonesome Luke. Amazed, he saw the grey man tighten his grip on his gun stock. The weapon whipped free. For one burning instant, Sunset thought Luke intended to fire upon him. Then he saw that Luke's eyes had gone beyond him to the doorway.

"Come on in," growled Luke. "It's just us girls."

Sunset turned. He saw Fred Firebank standing in the doorway. Cool as a block of ice, the hotel owner disregarded the gun.

"I heard a woman screaming here," he announced. "It is my duty to see that my guests are protected." He sniffed at Luke's gun. "Put up that hog leg," he went on, "and tell me what business *you* have in this room."

The angry glitter increased in Luke's hard eyes. Before Luke could reply, Sunset intervened. "One question deserves another," he drawled. "Suppose you tell me first just why one of your thugs brought these women up here and locked the door on 'em?"

Fred Firebank sneered. "I ordered you earlier to get

off my property," he snapped. "I'll say it again. *Get out!*"

"Not before you answer me. Why did you lock 'em in?"

"To protect 'em, you fool! You had started a shooting scrape in the lobby."

Sunset turned. He said to Dulcy. "Pack up! We are moving out."

Dulcy amazed him. She smiled upon Freddy. "But I don't wish to move," she said blandly. "I really believe that Mister Firebank will protect us here."

CHAPTER X

THE CHICAGO GIRL'S SUDDEN CHANGE OF FACE in this place which she had earlier thought a den of infamy amazed Sunset. The thought came to him that she was giving him the back of her hand, so to speak, because he had kissed her without an invitation. But she had stood close to him, just as now she was standing near the grinning Firebank. She had caressed Sunset's face with her soft breath, whispered sweet words of love into his big ear.

He cocked an eye, regarded her with sour wrinkles crinkling up his ordinarily homely but happy-looking face.

What most aroused his sudden bitterness was that Firebank, this hotel owner, who had so lately locked up Dulcy, was preening himself as he returned the smiles of the pretty daughter of the Chicago policeman.

Well, Sunset had to admit, Fred Firebank was a handsome fellow. Pink cheeks. Fluffy brown moustache neatly trimmed.

Freddy wasn't wearing his green eyeshade. Smiling upon the girl who had moved so near him, Fred raised his right hand delicately and patted his mousy brown hair. Curly hair, Sunset thought disgustedly, and remembered that his red thatch this moment was as tangled as rusty barbed wire.

Sunset felt the uncomfortable sensation of a lover, invited to spend the evening with his darling, who finds that she has broken the date to go out with his rival. She had appealed to him for help, revealed herself as a lady law. After all this, she had broken away from his protection, and, almost flamboyantly, accepted the protection of Freddy Firebank.

"A fellow would think," Sunset growled, "that a Chicago girl would know better."

"Chicago?" Freddy Firebank interrupted sharply glancing from Dulcy to Sunset. "I thought you girls came from Boston."

"Oh—so we did," she said breathlessly. "We—er— just passed through Chicago on our way West."

Firebank wasn't smiling now. There was a thin hard look on his mouth. He put up his hand to stroke his moustache. "You registered from Boston," he went on. "My understanding was that you intended to apply for jobs teaching in our Buckskin school."

"Mister Firebank," cooed Dulcy, "your understanding couldn't be any more right. You see—er—schoolmarms do get around. And they're apt to talk about where they've been and what they've seen. We told this gentleman," she nodded toward Sunset, "about the good time we had in Chicago. So perhaps he mixed that up with our real place of origin."

Firebank appeared deeply interested in the teachers' home town, Sunset reflected. What difference to Freddy where they came from? They were here, spending good money for a room in his second-class joint. But Sunset felt a slight qualm that he had almost revealed Dulcy as really not from Boston. However, he didn't care too greatly. Let her fawn on Firebank. That clothing dummy was smiling again serenely, plucking his moustache as if the thing were a harp.

Firebank turned his eyes again upon the dour deputy. His face became flinty. Sunset stared back but his mind was still upon Dulcy. It had come to him at long last that the girl might be playing a little game with Freddy. But she should have warned him. She hadn't. She had left him high and dry to ponder his next move. All he could think about—and that in an absent-minded way—was that Freddy's cheeks remained pink although the remainder of his face had now turned pale and cold.

"I don't intend to put on any more battles in front of these ladies," Freddy told the deputy. "I order you to get out of this room. *Off my property!* You have caused enough disturbance. You brag that you're an officer, sworn to enforce the law. *You* are the first to break it."

Sunset thought of a dozen arguments. But suddenly he didn't wish to trade angry words. Let Freddy believe he had won this round. If Dulcy was playing a game, let her play on.

"Well," said Sunset, and bent to take his bullet-torn hat from the floor where he placed it upon entering the room. "I want to enjoy the warm regard of all Buckskinners, Mister Firebank. So I will remove myself, pronto."

Firebank stepped into the hall to allow Sunset space to push through the door. As the deputy stepped past Dulcy, he gave her a sidelong stare. He thought she might answer with some sort of a signal, perhaps a wink of one bright eye. She never moved a muscle in her face. She said demurely, "We'll surely meet again. Thanks for your help."

Lonesome Luke proved a bird of different calibre. He was standing in the rear of the room. He picked up Mildred's long cloak which had been tossed over the end of the bed when she first entered the room. Luke opened it so that Mildred could slip her arms into the sleeves. Mildred was sitting on the edge of the bed, still watching all that went on with her weepy fearful eyes.

"Come on, Miss Smith," Luke said gently to her, giving the cloak an invitational twitch. "Slip into this. You're leaving this place with me."

Mildred arose slowly. She stood irresolutely, turning her head as she looked first into the eyes of Lonesome Luke, then toward Dulcy. And while Luke stood waiting and smiling—at least with a grimace upon his stern face that passed with Luke for a smile—Dulcy turned swiftly. She went to Mildred, and put her arm around her friend.

"She is staying with me," Dulcy insisted. "Thanks, Mister Luke. But she's not accustomed to wild spots like Buckskin. She'd be lost, away from me."

Luke's eyes became hostile. He gave Dulcy a hard stare. "She *may be lost* if she *doesn't* go with me," he stated flatly.

Sunset, standing in the hall, listening in with Firebank, heard the chill menace that rang in Luke's voice. But Dulcy, with quick colour flushing her cheeks, answered the gambler with a defiant toss of her head. She tightened her arm around Mildred protectingly. The Boston schoolmarm, confronted with another crisis, again wept.

"I wish," she sobbed, "that I could go home to Boston."

"Hush," whispered Dulcy. Then she hissed fiercely to Luke, but her words were meant for all of the listening men, "She's unstrung. Get out of here! All of you. Let me take care of her. Put her to bed where she belongs. Go on! *Get out*. Put that cloak down! *Hurry!*" She talked on and on. Her voice was muffling the frightening words that Mildred uttered as she now pressed her face against Dulcy's firm shoulder.

Luke broke in sternly. "I will hold you personally

responsible for her safety," he said to Dulcy. He spread the cloak over the foot of the bed. He turned and moved from the room into the hallway. At Sunset's side, he turned and challenged Firebank. "The same goes for you," he growled. Then, without another word, he started for the stairs to the lobby.

Sunset hesitated before he followed. He wondered now what move Firebank would make. But Dulcy swiftly took up the play. She helped Mildred to rest on the bed. Then, moving to the door in her easy graceful manner, Dulcy said to the two watchful men in the hall, "You will excuse us, I'm sure," and closed the door firmly in their faces. They heard the key turn in the lock.

In the hallway, Sunset had one last word for the hotel owner.

"Freddy—"

"Don't call me Freddy."

"Mister Firebank, then. I concur heartily with Lonesome Luke in his sentiments. I am leaving your dump—"

"No dump."

"Joint then. But I will sure return if you let anything happen to those Boston schoolteachers."

When he reached the lobby he discovered Luke seated in a chair near the stairway. Yum was over near the dining room entrance, sweeping the floor. He was very busy, humming a cheerful song in his peculiar lingo.

"Well," Sunset said, with a smile, "no more work for us here. I reckon. I'm amblin' down to Doc's place."

Luke looked up bleakly. "Go where you please," he returned. "I am registered here. I am not leaving this place at all."

Sunset continued to smile. "Well," he drawled, "in

that case, I should remind you that there's more than one way to get in and out of Mildred's room. There's an outside staircase at the far end of the hall. And for all I know—although this hotel looks like a two storey dive—maybe an attic to it."

Luke nodded.

"I thought perhaps," Sunset rambled on, "that you might be a trifle concerned over the murder of Happy Jack Coogan."

"That's *your* business," Luke said with grim finality.

"Well," Sunset said, turning away, "with you on guard, nothing is apt to happen to Miss Smith."

Firebank came down the stairway as Sunset started away from Luke. The hotel man stepped behind the desk, turning his neat back on the two men in the lobby. Luke's lips twitched, then closed tightly. Sunset went out into the street. He paused for a cautious survey. Plenty of openings where Slim Osage, One-Eared Budge and others could lay in wait.

No gun spoke. This was the dead hour in Buckskin. Sunset saw that the dusty street was wide enough for a twenty-team jerkline freight outfit to swing in the middle. The heavy tires of ore wagons had cut deeply into the soil. Up and down, the street was bounded by a motley array of weathered false-fronted plank shacks like Smith's Hotel, dirt-roofed log cabins, dingy canvas tents. Planks had been carelessly laid over low spots where water collected in pools when storms broke. Here and there, Sunset saw pole hitch racks, most of them in front of the camp's ten saloons. Up the street, toward the gravel banks of the gold fields, he saw a rambling plank structure with a big flapping canvas sign tacked to it.

"Firebank's Hall & Theatre," the sign read.

Sunset grinned wryly at this additional evidence of Freddy's business leadership. Then the grin vanished. His eyes turned sober when he saw faded black letters below Firebank's advertisement. He read off this information which ran:

"Formerly Coogan's."

Formerly owned by a murdered man who now lay in Doc's place. Coogan, who had asked the law to tame this camp, then been run out and beaten to death.

Sunset stood on the small plank platform that served as an entrance to the hotel. He estimated that he was about two feet above the level of the wide dusty street. There was room on the platform for the stage coach to unload passengers and baggage. Some boxes stood here marked with signs of Piute merchants. Perhaps they contained foodstuff for the hotel that was not carried in local stores. Old Smith had prided himself last year on, as he termed it, "setting a good table." Near the boxes there was also a large leather suitcase tightly strapped. And near it, a small neat wooden trunk braced with strips of metal.

Since Lonesome Luke wouldn't travel accompanied by trunk or suitcase, being the sort of lone ranger who would carry his change of clothing and extra decks of cards in a seamless grain sack war-bag, Sunset surmised the bag and the trunk belonged to the women guests of the hotel. He stepped over and saw on the end of the trunk, dim faded letters that reminded him of the weatherbeaten inscription on Firebank's theatre sign.

He bent his head to read two initials on the end of the trunk. So small and faded they were it was difficult unless a ray of light picked them out. Then he heard a dry voice, close to his ear, say in a whisper,

"She calls herself Smith. But it's M.B. painted on the end of her trunk."

Sunset turned swiftly and stared into the sardonic face of Luke.

"She signed the hotel register as Smith," the gambler went on. "But when I opened up her cloak, I see a tailor's label below the collar. M.B. were the initials."

Sunset pushed back his tattered hat. He hadn't had time yet to buy one unmarked by a bullet. Maybe there wouldn't be time. Nor the need for a new hat. Buckskin or bust!

"There's lots of Smiths out here," he drawled. "Maybe she had reasons to change her brand like others who come West."

"Maybe," Luke agreed. But he shook his head and said rather sadly, "She don't shape up like the sort of woman who'd need to change her name."

"No. That's a fact. Mildred from Massachusetts appears to be a right fine lady."

That remark drew from Luke one of his infrequent smiles. He stepped nearer to Sunset the better to study the initials on the end of the little trunk. "I aimed to speak to you in the lobby," he whispered, "about that label in her coat. But then this Firebank showed up. So I shut up. Now—"

"Well—"

"I am more convinced than ever that I better hang around this hotel lobby."

Sunset grinned. "But what about tonight? That is when the wolves prowl, Luke."

Luke turned on his heel and started back through the doorway. Sunset turned smiling to watch the gambler return to his guard over Mildred. There was something pathetic about the manner in which the soft little woman had won the love of Lonesome Luke.

"A man couldn't hardly say she won your heart," Sunset jested, "for you have the reputation of being plumb heartless."

Sunset never finished that remark. His eyes were off the wide street of Buckskin. But even in the throes of love Lonesome Luke was never off his guard. Those cold and wolf-like eyes were trained to watch flanks and front. Men said that Luke seemed to be able to see through the back of his narrow head. At any rate, he broke at the knees, drew his gun as he went down, and shouted to Sunset, "Bog your head!"

Warned, the deputy flung himself flat on the platform alongside the trunk—just as a rifle clanged up the street. A slug whanged into the end of the trunk not a foot from Sunset's head. He raked out his gun and looked for a target. The sudden thunder of Luke's gun drummed against his ears. A man who had stepped out from an alley mouth darted back into cover as Luke's bullet kicked up dust at his heels. The man was Slim Osage.

"Missed him," snarled Luke. "The hang of this gun's off some!"

CHAPTER XI

THE OUTBURST OF GUNFIRE DREW SOME WEAK-kneed interest in Buckskin. But after all, the wild camp was accustomed to such downbeat music, although not at this unseemly daylight hour. Sunset and Luke inspected the alley, found Slim's boot tracks where he had ducked through the alley, checked with the dozen or more apathetic Buckskinners who had gathered around. But Slim had made good his escape.

"He was handcuffed," Sunset declared. "I still got the key in my jeans."

"A blacksmith," said Luke, "could cut through the chain between the cuffs." The gambler was frowning as he inspected his pistol, then estimated the distance between the platform and the spot where Slim had stood to fire. "Not more than fifty paces," muttered Luke. "I should've marked him. But I was six inches to the right. This here gun don't throw correct at all."

Sunset pointed out that Luke had drawn and fired as he went to his knees. Luke wasn't satisfied. It was seldom he missed such a near target, moving, or braced like a post. Disturbed by the gun error, the gambler walked off, still muttering, to mount guard in the hotel lobby.

One of the Buckskinners wore the stained white apron of a butcher. "Who was Slim gunnin' for?" this man asked of Sunset.

"Me, I reckon."

The merchant shrugged. "Could be, since you're the fellow who called him a murderin' horse thief.

I heard about that. You'd be wise, young fellow, to get back to Piute while you're alive and kickin'."

"You in business here?"

"Yeah." The merchant jerked a thumb toward the hotel steps. "Run the butcher shop. There stands my boss."

Sunset swung around and thoughtfully regarded Fred Firebank standing on the hotel platform. Then he eyed the butcher. "I suppose," he said coldly, "that you sold him an interest. Needed a younger pard to help out."

The butcher's flabby-lipped mouth gaped. "How did you guess?" he gasped.

"Buckskin or bust!" chanted Sunset. Then he added, "Only it looks to me as if, since Firebank moved in, most of you Buckskinners have just gone busted,"

And leaving the staring citizens, he strode back to where Firebank waited.

"I heard shooting out here," said Firebank as Sunset shouldered past him on the platform.

"Your little friend, Slim Osage," said Sunset. "Tell him to raise his rifle sights next time. His bullet hit the schoolmarm's trunk." Then Sunset bent and picked up the trunk. It was not heavy. He balanced it on his shoulder.

"Now look here," Firebank began, "that trunk belongs to Miss Smith, one of the hotel guests. Put it back where you found it."

Sunset raised his hand and indicated the splinters where Slim's bullet had struck. "This trunk," he said, "goes with me."

"What for?"

"Evidence. This bullet hole here—"

Firebank laughed coldly. "You sure throw your

weight around," he scoffed. "What's a bullet or so in Buckskin?"

"This is evidence," Sunset said stolidly, "of assault with intent to commit murder on the part of Slim Osage."

Firebank laughed again. "All right," he said, "take it with you." He did not consider such evidence as worthwhile in this camp. "You *must* live," he drawled, "to have your day in court."

"Thanks for the kind thought," said Sunset, and went on down to Doc Backhammer's cluttered-up place of business which was housed in a rambling log cabin. What had inspired Sunset to carry away the trunk, however, was not the bullet hole but the dim initials on it. M.B. Mildred was the sister of murdered Mrs. Frank Flarity. And the victim's maiden name had been Hilda Beddows.

Dulcy had been careless to allow Mildred to display such clues to her identity. These gangsters were shrewd. They had known that Boston Charley was on their trail. How about the sister of the murdered woman?

Sunset felt that he ran some risk turning his back boldly on a hostile street as he carried the trunk down to Doc's log cabin office. But he gambled that the commotion touched off by the exchange of bullets had aroused too much curiosity. Ambushers preferred not to work where there were witnesses.

When the deputy lurched into the office, he found it occupied by Doc, a smooth-shaven fleshy old man, Jake, the coach driver, and the Buckskin agent of the stage line. They were seated around a table in the rear of the littered room and had apparently just finished a meal, for Sunset saw a coffee pot and dishes of grub on the board. Reminded that he had not eaten for some hours, he lowered the trunk to the floor and sat into the eating game.

Doc watched, then finally grunted. "About time you showed up. I sent word to the hotel that Jack Coogan had cashed in his chips right after the stage got in."

"I was hampered some," answered Sunset, reaching for a platter of fried deer liver and hashed brown potatoes.

The lean stage line agent nodded. "I explained that to Doc. I also flashed word to Piute about the holdup and trouble you're having here."

The stage line had installed a one wire telegraph line between Buckskin and Piute to transact its business. The agent, also a brass pounder, operated the line two hours each day unless emergency affairs such as holdups and murders arose. Most of the commercial messages, generally regarding mining claims, were sent out around supper time to accommodate late working miners.

Sunset poured some coffee. He asked Doc if he had ascertained the cause of Jack's death and was told that a hurried examination indicated a fractured skull. The drummer who had been hauled off the coach and shot to death had also been checked on by Doc.

"This dead passenger," Doc went on, "has been identified from papers found on him as Charley McBatt, a detective from Boston, Massachusetts. It seems his business here was to locate a wanted man named Frank Flarity. I told the agent to wire the Piute sheriff to that effect."

Sunset broke in. "So it was Frank Flarity or some of his friends who laid for the coach, knowing McBatt was on the way, stopped it, and killed him."

The agent added eagerly. "Sure looks that way. Here's some private dope. A wire came through here yesterday from down in the Medicine Bow country telling them up here to be on the watch for McBatt. He'd be wearing a derby hat and a white linen duster."

"Who got the wire?" Sunset asked, momentarily forgetting his food.

"One-Eared Budge of the Firebank gang."

Jake, the driver, growled, "So it was One-Eared Budge who did the killin'?"

Sunset frowned, shook his head. "Budge was a big man with a bushy red moustache. He might have been the fellow who stood guard though. No—I'll bet that the killer was this Flarity." He added, "If it was Flarity, we know that he has a real red face. The younger schoolmarm told us that."

Doc had listened silently but with a knowing look in his eyes. Now he spoke. "Red, you say?" And, rising, he went over to a work table. He returned and spread a linen duster on the table. He placed a thick forefinger on red spots around the collar. The spots stood out vividly against the white colour of the garment.

"Boston Charley's blood," snapped Sunset.

Jake, the driver, added solemnly, "The blood of an innocent man cries out for vengeance."

Doc Backhammer grunted and growled, "Trouble is—them spots aren't blood."

"Aren't blood?" Sunset voiced the amazement of Jake and the agent.

"Spilled blood don't stay bright red very long. Touch your finger to it, Sunset."

The deputy obeyed, then curiously examined his fingertip. It was stained bright red.

"That's war paint," said Doc. "I do a little assaying work for miners here. I know hematite of iron when I see it. Plenty in this country. Some places it carries high value. Wild Indians mixed it up with buffalo fat and bear grease and spread it on for war paint. Some places, it weathers out and turns into red dust. Other places you'll find the pure article."

He searched in the table drawer while Sunset, Jake and the agent further examined the red marks. Sunset believed they were the prints of the killer's hand when the latter had seized the protesting man to shoot him. Then he remembered that he had discovered similar spots on Jack's garments and, at the time, had believed they were Jack's blood.

Doc brought forth a round sandstone rock about the size and shape of a walnut. Then, with a small geologist's hammer, he cracked open the stone nodule. The sandy interior had washed away and been replaced by a small quantity of brilliant red powder. "Touch your fingers to it," Doc invited. "It's about as sticky as the rouge that the gals pretty up their lips with."

Sunset nodded. "I'll borrow this," he said to Doc, and put it in his pocket when Doc nodded his permission. Then Sunset again got down to business. He wanted to know what Doc thought of the hematite on the duster collar.

"Well," Doc drawled, "supposin' I was an outlaw who was called on in a hurry to disguise myself. If I happened to be in a red dust country like this one, what more simple than to pick up a handful and scrub it over my face? Of course I'd get some on my hands and, workin' in a hurry, would naturally transfer it to anything I touched. Or—if I was a real smart outlaw

—I might pack some of this war paint with me for such use."

Sunset listened silently. But his eyes narrowed when Doc grinned wryly and said, "Of course, there's a point that is in favour of this Flarity. If it was him killed this McBatt, why would he ride off leaving proof of the man's identity and who he was chasing on the body? No—a smart cooky, one smart enough to hide his features with Injun war paint, wouldn't do that. Not much."

Sunset saw instantly that Doc had made a big point in Flarity's favour. Of course he could have explained it. But that would have upset his plan of leading the Buckskin gang to believe that McBatt had been killed. He could have explained it by telling Doc that he had placed the papers in the dead drummer's pocket after he had talked over the plan with the Boston detective.

"So I reckon after all it was just a holdup," Doc ended.

"They got the strongbox," said Jake.

"But not much in it," added the agent. "The coaches coming this way seldom carry much value. Smart outlaws would have held up the outgoing coach which might have been carrying gold dust or bullion expressed to the Denver mint."

Doc listened; then he sat back in his chair and smiled smugly. "Well, whatever it was, I'm all through with it. I've served here as deputy coroner for couple of years along with doctorin' hosses and men, fillin' out mine location claims doing notary work and the like."

The agent nodded. "From what I hear, this place of your'n has been a money maker."

Doc nodded. "I know it. So I have decided to retire

and move to quieter surroundings. I move out of here tomorrow."

Sunset kicked back his chair. He stood up and pointed an accusing finger. "Nobody quits like that in a boom camp," he charged. "No—you are selling out like all these other yellow-bellied Buckskinners. Hotel man, butcher, baker—"

The angry charge did not ruffle Doc. He lounged in his chair, looking up at Sunset with that sly smile on his face, a grin, Sunset reflected bitterly, such as a cat would wear after swallowing a fat mouse.

"I have made a little stake," drawled Doc. "I aim to live long enough to enjoy it."

"The Firebank gang figured you were making money. So they have put the pressure on you, like they did on Old Man Smith and Jack Coogan and others—so-called good citizens who have hollered for the law to move in and take over; citizens too dang wrapped up in money makin' and fast profits to get together and do their own rat killing."

Doc at some time in his long and varied career had read the classics. "Lay on, MacDuff," he said approvingly.

"My name's McGee. You know it, you fat bag of suet. Your good friend, Jack Coogan, he was man enough to stand up to them. He lays there in your back room, dead. And you—you aim to move out, so Firebank's gang can take over and you can live to a ripe old age enjoyin' your ill-gotten gains." Sunset turned on his heel and spat on Doc's dirt floor. "Faugh," he snorted. "Faugh."

"Stick your head out the door to spit," Doc snapped, becoming angry.

"I will not only stick out my head but I will remove

myself entirely. There is something in here that smells ripe as a horse dead a week on the range."

"Get out," stormed Doc, lurching up from his chair.

"Don't forget you are still deputy coroner," charged Sunset. "You keep your eye on those two dead men. And this trunk I brought in."

"What about the trunk?"

"That's evidence. Slim Osage took a shot at me just now and hit the end of that trunk. It belongs to one of the schoolmarms. She's up at the hotel. Miss Smith."

Jake, the driver, nodded. "Yeah, I remember that trunk." He frowned. "Her name's Smith? But there's other initials on the trunk that don't match."

"Maybe she bought it second-hand," Sunset said carelessly. He stepped toward the door. He was bone-weary. He had expected to get a little sleep in Doc's place. But that was out.

Doc's angry command halted him on the threshold. "Wait," roared the deputy coroner. "Wait, you sassy red-headed pup."

"I got business up the street," snorted Sunset. He added wickedly, "Don't forget what I just said. You're a deputy coroner, under bond. Until you quit, you keep your eye on any evidence handed over to you of crimes committed. Men murdered, bullet-riddled trunks. *And so forth.*"

"And so forth," snarled Doc. "Well, young fellow, me lad, hear this. I'm my own man. Until I quit, I do my duty. Nobody in this camp, even the devil himself, interferes with old Doc Backhammer."

Sunset grinned and shrugged but without mirth. "Bah," he rasped, "you're yellow like all the rest. You're scairt out. But you got to stay and do your duty until you quit. Or it's apt to cost you some of that stake you got saved up. You aren't talkin' principle now. You are worrying about your money, like the rest of these Buckskinners."

With that, Sunset shut the door on Doc's anger. He stood outside the rambling cabin irresolutely. He had made a brave speech but it had been just words. He had been sent to tame a tough camp. And the men he had depended upon to aid him, every man jack, had thus far either refused to help or been killed off.

The agent and old Jake came out of Doc's place. The stage-line office was up the street, housed in a small square adobe building between Doc's shop and the hotel. Sunset had not the heart to ask for help from the agent or Jake. But now, at his wits' end, he followed the two men into the office. A plank counter divided the room. Passengers stood in the outer space to purchase coach fares or check baggage and express. Behind the counter, Sunset saw the agent's desk with telegraph instrument upon it, and nearby a steel safe in which valuable shipments could be stored until sent to Piute.

"It would be easy for some of the gang," he told the agent, "to drop in here when you're receivin' messages and listen in."

"Yeah," said the agent, "if they could read Morse code. But I haven't run into any brass pounders in the camp."

CHAPTER XII

SUNSET DIDN'T PRESS THE MATTER. He recalled hearing that organised gangs sometimes employed renegade telegraph operators to hang around railroad offices and stage depots and pick up advance clues on shipments of value. That would fully account for the Firebank gang being informed in advance of the coming of McBatt, also of the Piute law in the person of McGee.

By first drink time tonight, he reflected, the camp would know about the sudden deaths of Jack Coogan and Charley McBatt, the Boston detective. Such news always spread like wildfire on the frontier.

"If you have anything to send," the agent suggested, "file it now and I'll put it through to your boss when the wire opens at five o'clock this evening."

Sunset's first impulse was to send an angry bulletin that it might require more than the solid weight of one lone red-headed deputy to hold down the lid in Buckskin before a mayor was elected. Then he grinned and choked down his anger. He said carelessly to the agent as he strolled toward the doorway, "Just send my regards to the sheriff. Say I'm still on my feet and exerting tact."

"Tack," snorted Jake. "Hardtack like the soldiers eat?"

"Well," Sunset said judiciously, "I reckon it must be plenty hard to have any effect in Buckskin." And he opened the door and went on out into the street. He had eaten but his eyes burned from lack of sleep.

The town was very quiet now. But Sunset knew the lights of night would bring on plenty of noise and confusion. With Luke in the lobby, the two women would be safe while daylight lasted. A couple of hours sleep, Sunset thought, would brighten up his mind and perhaps relieve some of the soreness incurred in a morning of battles.

He considered going in boldly and registering for a room. But that would bring on another showdown with Fred Firebank. He preferred for the moment to let sleeping dogs lie while he followed suit. Slipping between the stage office and the hotel, he entered the alley. He had not been in the habit of beating hotel bills, but he had recalled the door at the end of the second floor hallway that opened out on a stairway leading down to this alley.

This was also the alley into which Slim Osage had ducked after taking his shot at Sunset. Assuring himself there were no witnesses, Sunset tiptoed up the narrow wooden steps that led to the second floor entrance of the hotel. The door was not locked. Softly opening it, he stepped into the hallway. The hall was darkening rapidly as the afternoon light faded away. But at the far end, Sunset marked the top of the stairs from the lobby, and also the location of the door opening into the teachers' room. He was half-minded to tiptoe down there, knock gently, and ask them if they were safe. But then he thought, half angrily, of the manner in which Dulcy had scorned his help and appeared so trustful of Fred Firebank. If he heard a scream or a scuffle, he'd go to her assistance. But not before.

He tried the first door but discovered it was locked. He crossed the hall and gently twisted the knob of the opposite door. The knob moved easily. The lock clicked from its slot. The door was open. For a long moment, Sunset stood listening intently. He was here without legal right. Firebank had ordered him off his property. Better perhaps to go his way and stay out of trouble as his chief had suggested.

As Sunset stood there in the fast gathering gloom of the hallway, it seemed to him that he heard faint sounds inside the room with the unlocked door. Sounds like the shuffle of feet across a carpet. He bent his ear to a door panel and listened tensely. He straightened up, shaking his head. All now was silence in the room. He had been mistaken. Perhaps a mouse, frightened by the opening of the door, had scampered away. But Sunset had to smile as that. Mice seldom made any noise. Certainly they ran as silently as death itself across carpets and rugs. So if he had heard anything at all, it had not been a mouse.

But though he sought to persuade himself that his senses had deceived him, that he really had not heard a sound in the room, yet he was cautious enough to draw his gun before he cautiously opened the door and stepped inside.

He stood a moment taking in is surroundings. A shaft of light through the window plainly revealed the contents of the room. It appeared to the deputy at first glance that this was a cut above the ordinary western hotel room. There was, of course, the brass-bound bed with its scanty bedding, battered wooden bureau and wash stand against the opposite wall. But a table had been added and two comfortable-appearing arm chairs. And in the far corner, curtains had been draped to shield garments, hung on a rack, from the eternal dust of Wyoming.

Sunset walked over to the table and saw by its contents that he could not hope to occupy this room for a cat nap. He picked up a silver-backed hairbrush, a comb similarly ornamented. There were various bottles, too, of hair oil, tonic and a big box of powder. Scented powder such as a barber used after he had given a customer a clean shave.

When Sunset examined the flashy hairbrush closely, he saw upon the back engraved initials entwined in a monogram. A moment's close study and he frowned. So far as he could read the engraver's artful work, the initials stood for F.F.

Sunset grinned. He turned around and whistled through his teeth. So, unwittingly, if the initials on the hairbrush meant anything at all, he had invaded the bedroom of Freddy Firebank. He recalled now that after Yum had prevented him from closely following Freddy up the lobby stairs, the man had vanished when he did reach the second floor. Presumably Fred had slipped into this—his private room.

Well, Sunset thought grimly, if Fred caught him here, he'd be in a pretty pickle, as an officer of the law in a man's private room without legal reason for being in it. Firebank could swear out a warrant charging Sunset with prowling or robbery.

If trapped here and thrown in jail, Sunset knew he'd lose all chance to tame Buckskin. The town would give him the horse laugh. Firebank and his bunch would glory in that. But the deputy couldn't resist the opportunity to inspect Firebank's room now that he had unwittingly invaded it.

Firebank, he soon discovered, was a neat and careful man. Whatever business he did, he placed no records in this room. Beyond clean clothing in the drawers and coats and trousers racked up in the bureau, there was nothing to show that Firebank was anything but a well-dressed law-abiding man.

Sunset searched hurriedly. He felt uneasy here, knowing that he could be caught if Firebank came up from the lobby. He walked over to the window and saw that if he tried to escape by that route, he must risk a drop from the second story to the earth. If he heard anybody approaching along the hallway, he would be forced to hustle out and run down the wooden stairway to the alley. They'd see him before he could get away.

But before he departed, Sunset whipped back the pillow and bedding at the head of the bedstead. Firebank kept a big calibre six-shooter there, a dully gleaming Colt. But that was not a suspicious thing. Probably every man in Buckskin slept with a gun under his pillow.

Sunset walked over and stood in front of the table where the fading sunlight gleamed on the silver-backed hairbrush. Above the table was a small mirror. Sunset saw his own face reflected in it. He frowned. Lack of sleep had ringed his eyes with black circles. There were also the bruises and scars of his fights. His red hair stood on end. He was dusty and unkempt as a range bum.

He reflected sourly, he couldn't pick up any shut-eye here. It looked as if he'd be forced to hunt up a patch of sagebrush and hit the hay in its cover. The ground was warm this time of year. He wanted to be wide awake when the camp came to lively life under the western stars.

Firebank's hairbrush—if it did belong to the hotel owner—fascinated Sunset. He had never seen miners and cowpunchers carrying such gaudy works of art around in their war sacks.

He examined his own red head again in the mirror. Bending forward, he picked up the brush. He told himself that he could also stand a shave and some of that slick powder in the box on the table. But that must wait until after the taming of the town. And then he would either pay the barber, or Doc Backhammer would foot the bill. Here on this range, deceased without friends were always shaved decently before burial, barbers charging double fees. Doc might be stuck twice. Sunset, leaning forward and about to comb his red hair with the fancy brush, grinned at the thought.

And then, behind him, he heard a slight sound, as though somebody had gasped or sighed. Instantly he recalled his caution before he entered this silent room. And then the thought flashed through his mind. Why was the room door unlocked? Surely Firebank—or whoever occupied the room—would not be so careless as to leave the door open. A prowler could enter and steal clothing and these silver brushes and combs.

Without replacing the brush on the table, the brush which he held in his gun hand, Sunset stuffed it back of his belt by its silver handle. That was to free his right hand instantly for action. He reached around and cleared his gun. He was still staring into the mirror. The gun draw hadn't taken more than the split part of a second.

Thus, staring into the mirror, he discovered from whence the sound had come. The glass reflected the curtain draped across the corner across the room. The curtains, Sunset had surmised, protected clothing from drifting dust.

Now, reflected in the mirror, he saw these curtains move slightly, as though stirred by a faint gust of air. But the door was closed, also the window. There was no draught within the room to cause curtains to move. No —*somebody was hiding* behind the curtains.

Sunset felt a cold chill run up his spine. For he stood with his back turned toward the curtains. And if whoever hid behind them was hostile, and had drawn a gun, then he could throw a shot before Sunset could whirl and fire a return bullet.

In his travels Sunset had occasionally seen trick gun experts in the theatre who could look into a mirror and hit a target by firing backwards. But he was not a magician with a gun. When it came to shooting, he preferred to face his mark. There was a moment that seemed hours to him—for he decided that whoever was hiding and watching through the narrow slit where the two curtains met—had seen his gun draw. That would alarm the hidden invader.

Better, Sunset thought, to be hung for a goat than a sheep. He half-whirled, dropping to his knees. He faced the curtains. His gun barrel flicked up. He was amazed that a bullet hadn't cut him down before he made this quick movement. A man like Slim Osage or One-Eared Budge would never have given him such a chance. No, any member of the Firebank gang would have shot him down, then asserted they had killed him because he was a hotel prowler.

When no hostile bullet pierced him, or roaring pistol drummed against his ears, Sunset arose warily. He tiptoed across the room. He held his gun high. With his left hand, he seized one of the curtains.

"Come on out," he ordered grimly.

When he tried to pull back the curtain, he felt

resistance. The person on the other side clung to it.

"Come out, I said," Sunset barked. He gave a violent jerk that tore open the curtain.

Sunset faced the person he had revealed so hastily. His mouth gaped, his eyes popped in amazement. He felt a hot flush warm his battered face. He found himself staring into the blue eyes of Dulcy.

What made Sunset flush was that Dulcy had removed her sedate travel costume. She now wore a frilly dressing-gown. She had gathered it hastily around her body and was holding it firmly anchored.

The glitter of Dulcy's eyes matched the bright flash of a diamond ring on one hand. Her face was white. Not with fear, Sunset saw at once, but with repressed anger. Her mouth might be invitingly red from rouge-stuff resembling the hematite in Doc's bit of stone— but she was biting her lower lip with her sharp white teeth. Under her dressing gown, her breast heaved with stormy anger.

Sunset stepped back awkwardly, almost falling over one of the arm chairs. He forgot too that he had taken off his hat to comb his hair and placed it on the table across the room. He reached up now to remove the hat that wasn't there in deference to the lady, found it was not there. He recalled that he held a cocked pistol in his right hand, eased down the hammer, started to thrust the gun behind his belt. He rammed the front sight against the silver hairbrush already tucked there. He glanced down hurriedly, tried to grab the brush, hurled it from him. In all his confusion, he finally succeeded in dropping both gun and brush. He got down on his knees to recover them.

Thus kneeling, he saw the feet of Dulcy peeping from below the hem of the silken dressing gown. The gown was a sort of red geranium colour, Sunset thought confusedly, like the pretty little flowers that grew wild in the mountains. Then he noted that Dulcy wasn't wearing slippers. She wasn't barefooted either. She was in her stockings. And one well-shaped foot was tapping the floor in anger.

When Sunset stood up slowly, his face was red. But now he was not confused. Wrath had also swept over him. He wasn't clumsy-handed as he thrust his gun into its holster. He stood facing the girl, holding the hairbrush in his left hand.

"You boxhead," Dulcy whispered, and he thought she had picked that talk up from Jake, the coach driver, for surely people weren't called boxheads in Chicago. No, that was entirely a Western expression. He wondered why she whispered, why she had hidden when he cautiously entered the room.

"I seem to have interfered with something that's none of my business," he said with a twist of his lips. His roving glance took in her dressing gown, her feet in stockings. She coloured hotly. She came from the compartment. He saw behind her, swaying on racks, masculine garments. She had hidden there when he stole into the room. A sigh had betrayed her. Also that faint movement she had made attempting to hold the curtains together. So ran the luck, good or bad, for men and women.

Sunset walked over to the table and picked up his bullet-scored hat. He slanted it down on his head. Then he turned to face her with a dry smile on his face. "I'll get out," he drawled. "From your looks, I am in the way."

She came across the room swiftly. She had clenched her right hand into a fist. She looked as though she would like to give Sunset a bunch of fives right in his front teeth.

"What are you thinking?" she flamed—but still she kept her voice low. "Intruding? Well—you certainly are a prowler. The way you tried to get away with that hairbrush. Hand it over," She reached out her hand and he gave the brush to her.

"I wouldn't need the thing," Sunset said with a shrug. "A sport like Freddy Firebank might use it, but not me."

"So you know that you're in Firebank's room?" she flared.

"Don't you?" The question was an ugly one. She resented it by drawing back her right arm for a full-armed swing. But then she thought better of it. She let her arm drop. The colour faded from her face. She said dully, "Well—if you judge everybody by appearances—then I suppose mine are against me."

"I worried about you before," he said. He backed toward the door. "But not now. You seem to know your way around Firebank's hotel. So—I'll be seeing you later." He bobbed his head but he didn't take off his hat politely as he stepped out into the hallway.

He went down the outside stairway into the alley. He found a patch of sagebrush outside the town limit and stretched out for two hours sleep. His last thought as he drifted off was that Dulcy should have locked the door when she entered Freddy's room.

CHAPTER XIII

THE COYOTES IN THE RED HILLS THAT SURrounded the camp were saluting the evening star with howls when Sunset rubbed sleep from his eyes and crawled from his hard bed in the sagebrush. He found his way over to the creek which murmured along between clumps of willows. The starlight was reflected in the cold water as he knelt, removed his hat, and rubbed the grime off his face. The reflection from the water reminded him anew of the mirror in Firebank's room. Sunset thought bitterly that he wished he had not fooled around that room, staring into the mirror, worrying about his trail-worn appearance.

What a man didn't *know* didn't hurt him. That was Sunset's code. Of course, the Chicago girl was her own boss. He held no claim on her. But she had been so lively and sweet. She had stood up for him bravely during the fight in Happy Jack's place. He wiped the cold water off his face with his neck scarf. How he wished now that he had not found her hiding in Firebank's room, all togged up in a fancy silk gown. And wearing diamonds.

Maybe he'd been fooled by Dulcy's story that she was a Chicago policeman's daughter, that she was also a lady law. Her protective attitude toward Mildred might be just the stall of a clever female crook.

When Sunset had washed up, he made a wary circle before he entered the camp's main street. All the prospectors would now be in from their claims. Some would be blowing in gold dust they had taken from pockets along the valley. Others would be borrowing the price of supper. All the human hawks, vultures and wolves who preyed on the lucky ones, would be emerging from their hideouts for the night's harvest.

Firebank's gang had good connections here. He remembered his talk with the agent and the latter's surmises that warning had been wired to the gang of the approach of Boston Charley and Sunset.

He halted at the far end of the street. This was where the larger shacks petered out into occasional huts and tents in tin can littered suburbs. Not far distant up the valley from where he stood, oblongs of yellow lamp light marked the front windows of Doc Backhammer's cabin, on beyond it, the stage office, and the hotel entrance.

Oil flares flamed in front of the hall which Firebank had taken over from Happy Jack Coogan. Sunset frowned at sight of a crowd gathering in front of the place. Strains of brassy music drifted to his ears. It sounded as though Firebank was using a band to draw a Buckskin audience to his theatre.

Sunset twisted his lips in a sneer. Two men lay murdered in Doc's shop but gay music entertained the careless Buckskinners. In all that cold-hearted camp, not a man had volunteered to stand up for the law.

The deputy had half a mind in this bitter moment to go to the stage line agent, request him to wire in his resignation to the sheriff. Then he'd get a horse from the public livery, ride off. Let Firebank and his gang take Buckskin for better or for worse.

What chilled his heart, far more than lack of support from such men as Doc Backhammer and old Smith, was his latest meeting with Dulcy. Had she played him for a fool? Was her story of coming West to run down a murderer just a clever ruse to gain his confidence? Was she, in reality, a clever agent for the gang?

What was that she had said as they parted in Firebank's room? That appearances were certainly against her. Well, what could she expect? A girl arrayed in a silk gown, hiding in a man's hotel room.

Gazing up the noisy main street of the boom camp, Sunset clenched his hands into hard fists. Just then he wished he could face sneering Fred Firebank and beat him to his knees. Then anger simmered down. A faint doubt came into the deputy's feverish mind. Perhaps after all he was misjudging the girl. He could not forget the actions of her companion, the weeping Mildred. Mildred certainly was not an actress. Her fear and tears had been genuine enough. Her every action indicated that she trusted Dulcy to the limit.

Sunset didn't wish to venture out into the light without taking precuations. He did not forget that Slim Osage was free, armed, and alert. He had escaped wearing steel cuffs. Sunset carried the key to the bracelets with him. But a blacksmith could have cut the short chain that ran between the cuffs. It would take more time and prove a difficult task to remove the cuffs without the key. But Osage would be free to handle a gun, as he had demonstrated earlier when he put a bullet into Mildred's trunk and then escaped Lonesome Luke's gun.

Expert gunmen like Lonesome Luke never fired by eye aim. They directed their pistols by the feeling of balance which they called "hang." When they drew on their target, it was as though they pointed a trigger finger at the mark. Instinctively they knew by the way the gun fell into line when the weapon was dead on the target. The moment they felt that "hang," they fired—and generally hit the mark. If a gun got out of "hang" they said it "threw" high or low. Sunset did not class himself as an expert. But he knew that men like Luke stood for hours in front of mirrors, simulating firing. Thus they became accustomed to the "hang" of their particular gun.

One of the common ways which ruined the "hang" of a gun was to beat the barrel on an opponent's head. Sunset wondered if Luke had earlier in the day pistol-whipped an enemy.

Sunset glanced toward the hotel entrance. He hoped that despite the out of hang gun, Luke was now in the lobby, keeping guard over his beloved schoolmarm from Massachusetts. Miss Mildred Smith whose name did not match the initials in her cloak or on her trunk. In reality, according to Dulcy's account, Mildred Beddows, sister of the murdered wife of Frank Flarity.

Sunset tightened up grimly. The sister of the murdred woman—and if Frank Flarity discovered her—she would soon join her sister in the grave.

While he cogitated, the deputy had kept carefully hidden in the inky shadows cast by trees growing along the broad road which entered Buckskin. Miners from cabins down the creek were now walking or riding up into the brightly lighted centre of the camp. Heading for the ten saloons, roistering cafes, toward the noisy crowd listening to Firebank's brass band.

The paths and occasional plank walks further on up the valley were also crowded with the hurrying throng. Sunset saw them plainly enough under the lights; miners in muddy garments, pretty girls in high-heeled slippers, sleek tinhorns hastening from supper to various games of chance which they ran in back rooms. Riders were in town too from the ranches. Here and there, ponies stood slouching in front of saloons.

As Sunset took in the sights, a knot of horsemen

galloped past him heading straight up town. He marked them closely as they dashed past; a half-dozen wide-hatted men bending over the necks of their ponies. A six-gun flashed in the light as the leading rider struck the main street. A rattle of shots saluted Buckskin; and a high wolfish yelping.

Sunset surmised the riders were cowboys, paid off and riding into town for a spree. Then he frowned. He had caught a glimpse of the leader. He wasn't sure but he was *almost* certain that the man was One-Eared Budge.

The thought that he had seen Firebank's henchman, the man tied up with the gang, spurred Sunset into action. He forgot his angry plan of wiring a resignation to the sheriff. While Budge, Osage and Firebank ruled Buckskin, he would not quit. Sunset would have laughed at the thought that pride and principle spurred him onward. But that was what now stirred his heart. There always came some point in life where a man must stand his ground or run like a coward. Sunset turned and hurried up the street. He clung to the shadows, keeping narrowed eyes on the receding horsemen. They were now nearing the gaudy theatre front.

As Sunset approached Doc's place, he saw a man stroll from the hotel into the street. Passing Doc's doorway, coming nearer the man, Sunset saw by the flapping garments that it was one of the Chinks from the hotel. Yum or the relative who had found Yum a job.

As Sunset recognized the peaceful Chinese, the horsemen made a wide sweep around the far end of the street. They lined out, coming toward Sunset. Some of the riders began firing guns toward the stars. Their loud, mocking shouts shrilled above the booming clatter of pony hoofs. Sunset had before this seen celebrating cowboys in town, shooting things up for fun. Generally they were not hostile, just filled with the joy of life and hard liquor.

He stood not twenty-five long horse jumps from the hotel and the Chinese who had paused alongside the road when the first rider raced past. This was the man who resembled One-Eared Budge.

The bright lights assured Sunset that it was indeed the gunman who had put a bullet hole in his hat.

Budge reined down his galloping pony so abruptly that the cayuse's hoofs dug into the hardpan. Then, with the swift skill of the rangeman, Budge bent, freed the coil of rope strapped to his saddle swell. His five men came to a clattering dusty halt. They milled around Budge as he shook out a lariat noose. Their laughter and whooping arose loudly.

Sunset, running ahead, heard a rider shout, "What's up, Budge?"

Budge brawled back. "There stands the Chinese who cooked for Happy Jack!"

Yum heard and tried to flee. Before he could scuttle off, Budge's noose whipped out. It settled down over Yum's bobbing head.

With a loud laughter, Budge and his men sat their horses. Budge jerked Yum off his feet. The cook went down fighting, clawing at the strangling noose. In another instant, Budge would spur his horse down the street, dragging Yum to death.

Before Budge could throw spurs into his mount, Sunset rushed out into the street. The five riders with Budge carried guns. There was not time now to worry about that. He must act instantly to save the life of the helpless man clawing impotently at the noose around his neck.

"Budge!" Sunset shouted. "Hold your horse up! Or I'll kill you!"

The threat amazed Budge. This was his camp. Who dared to interfere with his pleasure?

Budge swung his white-eyed pony. He confronted the deputy. Budge's men followed his action, thrashing around like a school of hungry sharks.

Rising in his stirrups, Budge looked over the ears of his pony. The man had completely forgotten his deadly fun with the cook. His rope had slackened. The intended victim sat in the dust, working frantically to free his neck.

Law and lawless stood in plain sight under the lights of Buckskin. Not ten paces separated them. The lone law. For behind Budge were grouped five armed men. All awaited a signal from their chief. Who was this pilgrim who had dared to call their hand?

"Sure as I live!" roared Budge, his wiry red moustache flaring. "It's that Piute law! *Sunset McGee!*"

And with that, Budge yelped harshly, "Ride over him, boys!"

Spur steel flashed. Guns tilted upwards. Five men gathered up reins to charge Sunset.

He would not retreat. He stood with his legs braced as though facing a big wind. He saw Budge yell, jerk a gun, drive his pony forward. Sunset's gun began an iron clanging as if it were a firebell.

Budge flopped over his saddle horn. His maddened cayuse swerved from the flash and roar of Sunset's gun. Roaring and bucking, the horse whirled, and smashed back through the line of five riders.

Budge was carried out of the fight still in his saddle. Where he went, Sunset had no time how to discover. He found himself the centre of a breathless smoky fight.

A pony with white eyes glaring above red flaring nostrils, reared over him. A hoof fanned his face. A gun blast deafened him. He lurched aside to dodge the mad horse. He fired, saw the rider tumble from his saddle and hit the street with a smash.

Another yelling horseman drove in, striving to knock down the deputy. Sunset felt a sudden jarring blow against his short ribs. He was sent rolling from the street. Desperately, he clung to his gun, but despairing that he would live to throw another bullet.

Then, from somewhere nearby, Sunset heard confusedly the roaring reports of another gun, not the flat barking of hand guns but the bull-bellow of a big black powder gun. A buffalo rifle.

The forlorn hope struck Sunset's heart that at last a man of Buckskin had decided to help the law. Sunset staggered up. The buffalo gun had broken up the charge. Two riders were down in the street, also a feebly kicking horse. A dismounted rider fled across the street to cover. Sunset tried to fire. Before he could snap the trigger, the buffalo gun boomed. The fugitive flung up his arms. He fell flat, and didn't kick once after.

From the hotel entrance, a sixgun was spitting. Sunset risked a bullet and turned. He saw Lonesome Luke standing on the porch. Luke snapped down his gun. This time his Colt hung correctly. Another rider slid off his pony.

Sunset also saw Yum crouching at the feet of Lonesome Luke.

CHAPTER XIV

Of all Buckskin, only the tinhorn gambler, the man run out of the county seat, dared aid the law. Lonesome Luke, the man who had said cynically that the law could skin its own cats. Well, he stood there now, boldly with balanced gun gripped in hard fist. And he had just shot the daylights out of one of Budge's gang. He loomed protectingly as a rock over the lone and frightened Chink.

Sunset felt breathless from the kick in his ribs. Dust coated his face, choked and blinded him. He gripped his smoking gun but his legs were beginning to betray him. He wobbled out into the street striving for a last shot at the remaining horseman. From his flank came a wheezy yell. "Hit the grit, you fool! Get out of bullet line!"

One rider of Budge's contingent remained. He was a bold man. Perhaps he believed he could never ride out of this fight. Seeing the staggering deputy, he flung his pony about and rode straight down on Sunset. Vainly, the latter attempted to evade the rush of the horse. Struck by a slashing forefoot, Sunset was hurled into the hardpan. The bloody grit of Buckskin. He did not see as he fell, that mighty buffalo gun boomed and the man who had charged him, plunged off his pitching horse.

Nor did Sunset discover how the fight had ended until he at last came out of the black world into which he had been plunged. His throat and stomach felt as though they were on fire. He struggled up, believing he still held his gun, and outside surrounded by a swirl of maddened riders.

He was forced down on his back. He felt a rough hand at his throat. He choked. Then came a draft of heat that burned its way to the pit of his stomach.

The searing agony brought Sunset out of his feverish delirium. He blinked his eyes painfully. A cruel light blazed into his face. His wits cleared slowly of the fog of battle. He discovered that he was staring up into the eyes of Dock Backhammer.

"You boxhead!" Doc stormed, "I told you to get out of bullet line."

Sunset choked. "So—so it was you with that buffalo gun. You—you saved my life."

"I told you before I'm still deputy coroner," snorted Doc. "No pack of varmits can jump a Chink or even a sassy deputy sheriff while I hold office. Now, lay down there while I spike you up with some more tonic."

"Tonic?" gasped Sunset. "It—it's about burned out my windpipe! Is it horse medicine, Doc?"

"Hoss medicine nothin'. This is some of that Peerless Painkiller stuff brought to camp by the poor drummer they killed. I'm just tryin' it out to see how it works."

"Gah," grunted Sunset. "It—it sure works." He squirmed over and found that he had been laid out on one of Doc's work tables. Perhaps the table that had also served for Doc's post mortem checks on the two dead men.

When at last Sunset could look around, he discovered that Jake, the driver, was guarding the front door with a huge black powder rifle. It was one of those Sharps Big Fifties, Sunset judged. A gun that would knock down a bull six hundred yards off if held right on the target.

Sunset sat up and swung his legs off the table. He felt

weak and watery but didn't fancy resting any longer on an autopsy table. "Thanks, boys," he mumbled gratefully. He found speech difficult. His upper body felt as though every bone had been broken.

Doc stood in the centre of the room with the black bottle in his hand. He was examining the label by the light of a turned down oil lamp which he had placed on the table. Above the table on which Sunset sat, the reflector of another lamp cast down a harsh glare. Except for this one shaft of light in the rear of the room and the dim pool of light on the table, the remainder of the room was shadowy. Jake, the old driver, crouched by the front doorway holding the rifle. Sunset saw that blankets covered front windows. Then to his ears came a noise outside, a confused deadly sound which at first had no meaning.

He slid off the table. The moment he felt his heels strike the floor, he stood up. And almost fell over. There seemed to be no strength left in his legs below the knees. Only by bracing himself against the table, could he stand up.

Doc slapped the bottle down so violently on the table that the lamp almost upset. Moving swiftly for so big a man, Doc reached the table. He flung his arms around the swaying deputy, raised him up as though he were a child, and laid him flat on his back.

"Stay there!" Doc boomed angrily. He peered down into Sunset's face. "What in the devil's come over you? You're weak as a starved kitten. Lay there. Rest and get back your strength."

Sunset stubbornly tried to prop up on an elbow. Doc put his hand hard against Sunset's face and shoved him down again. This time he held him there despite feeble struggling. "You're tired out," he growled. "Also that pony kicked you in the ribs. Winded you. No bones busted. But you can't move around just yet."

Sunset twisted his sore face into what he hoped was a coaxing grin. "Doc—I—I can't lay here! I got work to do."

Doc jeered. "What work?"

"Give me a shot of whisky, Doc. Or even some more Painkiller. Somethin'. Then I'll walk uptown under my own power."

Doc waited a moment to assure himself that Sunset would repose quietly on the table top. Then he walked over to where the black bottle glittered dully in the shade of the lamp. He picked up the bottle and shook it until Sunset heard the gurgling of the contents. "This stuff," Doc announced, "is nothing but a cheap grade of rotgut likker. Got a red hot taste because it's so young. No age to it. I suppose this Boston Charley just faked it up as medicine to make good his play that he was a drummer. Well—it's strong p'izen stuff, all right. It'll kill pain. A quart of this taken in a hurry and your troubles would be all over forever."

"Well—a couple of shots, Doc, just to put some life in my legs. They feel numb from the knees down."

Doc took the black bottle. He sauntered over to a littered desk against the wall, picked up a pony glass, and poured out a drink for Sunset. "No chaser," he announced, coming over and handing the drink to the deputy. "We got to save our water."

"Save your water?" Sunset reached for the drink. He frowned over it. "Why, there's the creek just beyond your back door."

Doc shrugged and answered grimly, watching the deputy with narrowed glittering eyes. "Drink deep," he ordered. And as Sunset raised the glass under his nose and almost gagged as the fiery odour assaulted his nostrils, Doc said, "They're all around this house."

"All around?"

"Sure. Firebank's gang. They got here fifteen minutes after Jake and me dragged you in from the street. What do you suppose all that noise is outside?"

For a moment, Sunset forgot his drink. He had propped himself up on one arm to take the drink. Now he listened tensely and what he had thought of before as a confused murmur now resolved itself into the hurried muttering voices of men, the shuffle of boots on the street, occasional sounds, too, that came from the sides and the back of Doc's place.

"They want you bad," Doc explained quietly. He frowned. "Aren't you ever going to take that shot of p'izen? You asked for it."

"Dutch courage," jeered Sunset. His heart felt cold at the thought that he had become the object of mob vengeance and that this fat man and old Jake—men of peace—had become involved with him. Better, though, to keep up nerve and courage. Stiff upper lip, some folks termed it. He smiled at Doc, opened wide his mouth and tossed down the shot of Painkiller. The stuff burned its way down to about belt level. The pathway it made down his gullet felt as though he had just swallowed a red hot tenpenny nail. The tears came to his eyes. He had to sit up on the table to catch his breath.

Doc smiled grimly. He removed the empty glass from Sunset's grimy claw. He turned half around to replace it on the desk. Window glass tinkled. A gun barked just outside the cabin. The pony glass held by Doc suddenly flew into a dozen shimmering pieces. The bullet that had been fired through the front window without any particular target in view, the bullet that had hit the glass and by scant inches missed blowing away part of Doc's valuable right hand, smacked into the rear wall of the office. Gyp plaster fell to the floor where it had entered.

While Doc stood there with a sort of foolish look on his round face, staring pop-eyed at the rim of the glass which he still clung to, old Jake leaped to the window through which the bullet had entered. He was about to drag aside the blanket which now bore a neat black hole in it when Doc came to life. He threw down the bit of glass and leaped toward Jake roaring for him not to be a boxheaded idiot.

"They're shootin' in here!" yelped Jake. His whiskers quivered. The polished brown stock of the old Sharps was almost at his shoulder for a return shot. "Dang their dirty hides! Why, that bullet was shot from close up!"

"I know. I know," Doc sputtered. He had reached Jake's side. He took the gun away from the old driver. "If you had got mad and lost your head and jerked down that blanket, they'd fire a volley in here. Maybe put all of us out of action. No! That bullet came from close up. I heard the gun distinctly. Just outside the window. Wait a minute! Listen!"

The cabin occupants listened intently. Even Sunset forgot the burning sensation in his stomach. The mutter of voices outside had died down suddenly. Not even the shuffle of nervous boots could be heard. And then, sharp and distinctly, a voice outside was raised.

"This is me, Fred Firebank! I'm just outside your house, Doc. I fired through the window to warn you. If you value your hide, you will throw down your gun and turn over that fellow, McGee."

Doc carefully placed the butt of the Sharps on the floor. He stood listening to Firebank's harsh high-pitched voice coming from just outside the bullet-riddled front window. Jake, the driver, stepped back to the centre of the room. He leaned against the table that held the low-turned lamp. There was an angry look on Jake's face. He reached back and took a plug of tobacco from his hip pocket. He put one corner in his mouth and began to worry off a good hearty chew.

Sunset, for his part, was sitting upright again on the table with legs dangling over the edge. He looked first toward Doc, then moved his eyes to Jake. He saw the big rawboned driver wedge his back teeth into his chew, dust off the end of the plug, and carefully put it back in his hip pocket. Then Jake turned his head and looked solemnly at the deputy. A long, long look that seemed to the deputy to enter into him and search deeply into his heart. Sunset stared back at Jake. He was waiting for Doc's answer. So was Jake.

These two rough men owed nothing to Sunset McGee. A few hours before, like a hotheaded kid, he had told off Doc and gloried in it. He had sneered at the old man because he loved peace and would sacrifice a good business in Buckskin to live in peace. And Jake—what about Jake? He earned around fifty dollars a month at the hard monotonous job of driving a coach back and forth between Buckskin and Piute. In winter blizzard and in burning heat of summer. Jake made his daily drive of sixty long, long miles. Certainly old Jake owed nothing to Sunset McGee. And what did Jake owe to the law and the society that the law was supposed to protect? Old Jake was not a millionaire. It was quite likely that when the time came for him to die, unless friends rallied around, he would fill a pauper's grave.

Sunset slid his legs slowly toward the floor. Cautiously he put down his feet. And this time, being wary, he clung to the table before he put his solid weight upon his legs. He was glad that his knees didn't buckle. He stood there a moment, head whirling, as he fought for balance. And then he knew he could move some, but not far nor swiftly, under his own power. At least, he would not meet the enemy, flat on his back.

Doc turned his head and said quietly to Sunset, "Darn you, I told you to stay on that table."

Sunset essayed an apologetic grin that hurt the side of his face. "I can handle myself some, Doc."

Again came the strident shout of Fred Firebank. "Doc—you and Jake come out! Unarmed! And you'll not be hurt! All we want is that fellow, McGee!"

Jake had turned his head away to listen to Firebank. Sunset marked the movement of Jake's big jawbones as his back teeth worked on the chaw. Then the chewing ceased momentarily while Jake listened to Firebank. After that, it resumed and quite calmly. A man would have thought Jake was chewing tobacco and taking his time to it while he watched a minstrel show.

Doc Backhammer answered the mob chief for the first time, craftily, "Why do you want McGee? He never did anything to you."

"Tonight he just about murdered One-Eared Budge. There's other men dead—and their horses. Shot down in cold blood here on our main street. Killed by this bloodthirsty young gun shark from Piute."

Doc turned and cracked his face in a thin smile meant for Sunset. Then he asked another question of the mob leader. "You mean he didn't kill One-Eared Budge?"

"No. But Budge is shot through the body and not apt to live out the night."

"Bring Budge around after he cashes in," Doc invited heartily. "I'll call an inquest to sit on him, same

E*

as was done for Jack Coogan and that Boston Charley, the detective."

Firebank was silent a moment. Then he shouted angrily. "Quit joshin', Doc. Budge ain't dead yet. But others are. This McGee started a fight on the boys when they were just funnin' around."

"Yeah," Doc cut in heavily, "just havin' fun chokin' your cook to death. Whatever become of the cook, Fred? I hear he was good on meat and spuds."

"To heck with the Chinaman. Who cares about a Chinaman? He's quit camp cold. The boys wouldn't have hurt him, just drug him some. They blamed him for buttin' in on 'em in a little rampage they had with this McGee at Coogan's ranch this mornin'. But McGee took it as an excuse to shoot 'em all up and kill two or three of 'em. There's fifty citizens out here, Doc, all good men and true. They've set me up as leader tonight. We will let you and Jake go free. But unless you come out and let us get out paws on McGee, we will burn you out. Roast you to death, or string you up with McGee. You got five minutes, Doc, to make up your mind."

CHAPTER XV

Doc turned the buffalo gun over to Jake who resumed guard at the front of the cabin. Doc sauntered back to where Sunset sat on the edge of the table. An old clock hung on the side wall and Doc glanced solemnly at its face. "Five minutes," he drawled, "can be long as a lifetime or short as a bulldog's tail."

Sunset shrugged and said to the old man, "I'm sorry I spoke out of turn this afternoon. I was some riled up. Five minutes is long enough for me. You go over there and tell Firebank you'll take his offer."

"We save this shack and our hides? You walk out to Firebank and his bloodthirsty boys?"

"You two saved my bacon once tonight. It's not up to you to keep up the good work." Sunset touched his gunbelt then gestured toward Jake and the old gun. "If you'll let me have that cannon. I figure I can make quite an impression on Fred and his bunch before they wipe me out."

Doc sat down on a chair by the table. He could face the busily ticking clock. "Plenty time left," he observed. Then he turned a wise eye on the deputy. "And what would you win by allowin' Firebank to wipe you out?"

"They wouldn't hurt you, Doc. Nor Jake."

"Two minutes gone," sighed Doc, leaning back in his chair, "and no wisdom as yet. Now I been kickin' around this vale of tears and misery right on to sixty years. Never found out much but this. Older I get life seems sweeter to me. Don't know how it seems to you young pups that like to bulge out like you did tonight and dang near get your head kicked off by a bronk."

Sunset set his jaw stubbornly. "Budge was getting ready to choke that poor Chinaman to death. I had to do something."

"So you lunge out bold as anything and give 'em a show at you. Furthermore you waste time by givin' Budge a moment for careful reflection."

"What would you have done, Doc? Let 'em kill the Chinaman?"

"No. I would have stood there in the shadows. I woulda kept my big mouth shut, up with my gun, and knocked Budge kickin' for his saddle."

"It doesn't seem right to shoot a man without warning."

Doc gave the deputy a sour look. "You are what the Injuns call brave white. Which means that for some obscure reason called sportsmanship you will run foolish risks knocking out a human wolf like Budge. Do you suppose he'd give you a show for your white alley? Or Firebank? Or any of that gang? That's the reason they have bossed this camp. They strike without warning. A man who's at outs with them never knows, day or night, when the roof may fall in on him."

"Just the same, an officer of the law—"

"—is supposed to step in and get his fool self killed off. And what for?" Doc turned and nodded toward the closed door, the blanketed windows. "There are fifty men outside, a mob. Likely they are all stoked up on Firebank's bad likker. If you walked out there with a gun in each hand, you'd hardly get a chance to shoot once."

"All I ask is that *once*. I can at least get Firebank."

Doc looked at the clock. "Three minutes," he announced. "And nothin' to show for it except bullheadedness. Now me and Jake didn't haul you in here just to show we're heroes. Before we ventured out there to help you, we made dang sure with the buffalo gun that the odds was in our favour. And now—havin' bought into this game—we don't figure to lose it none. So—"

Sunset put his boots down on the floor. He faced Doc, shaky but determined. "I won't let you two men get hurt over me," he said defiantly. He drew his gun. He didn't line it on Doc. But his intent was plain. If forced to, he would command Doc and Jake to put him out of the besieged cabin.

Doc seemed to disregard the gun. He gave the clock another look. "Four minutes," he tolled off. "Put up that gun. I doubt if you'll need it."

"I intend to go out of here."

"We'll *all* go out," said Doc.

The sharp command of Firebank came through the window. "Five minutes is up, Doc, What's the answer?"

Doc got up from his chair. He winked at the deputy who had now turned a sort of ashy colour. It wasn't pleasant to contemplate walking out, even with a pair of guns, into the hands of a bloodthirsty mob. Sunset watched old Doc move to the blanketed window through which Firebank had fired and through which he had issued his commands.

"Freddy," bawled Doc, "I told you before I would leave this camp at my own sweet pleasure. That still stands good. I will come out and Jake with me when I feel like it. And when I come, this John Law from Piute will be with me."

"You're a fool, Doc!" shouted Firebank. "Our next move will be to set fire to your cabin."

"These logs are green," rejoined Doc. "It'll take time

for 'em to catch. And there's a dirt roof. It won't burn at all."

"When you begin to blister on your fat legs, Doc, you'll talk different. Well—I did all I could for you—" And a torrent of shouts and a blast of gunfire shut off the sound of the mob leader's harsh voice. Some of the bullets cracked the window panes and drilled holes through the blankets. Some thumped into the stout panels of the door. Jake spat angrily and wanted to return the fire but Doc told him quietly not to waste bullets. "One bullet against fifty won't do much good," said Doc.

Listening to the shouts and the gunfire, Sunset was suddenly gripped by wild unreasoning anger at the contrary old man. "This deal is none of your affair!" he stormed. "No call for you and Jake to roast on account of me!"

Doc was waddling amiably around the dim room with a small black leather case in his hand. Into it he was putting various articles from table and desk. He even walked around his work table and over to the wall where Firebank's bullet had drilled into the plaster. With a knife, he removed the gleaming bit of lead. He bounced it up and down in his hand. Sunset came around after him, intent on arguing Doc into allowing him to quit the cabin. The sight of the bullet made him remember the slug that had come from Hilda Beddows' head and which Boston Charley had handed over to him as a clue in the case. He took out the pillbox, opened it, and showed Doc the murder slug nestling on a wad of cotton. The ceiling lamp revealed it plainly.

"You know," Doc said suddenly as he took the slug from its bed, "I'm a sort of a gunsmith. Have worked on guns, and also loaded ammunition for years for the boys." He placed the murder slug on his palm alongside the bullet he had just dug from the wall. "I'd swear," he went on, "that they match. Outside of a few minor scratches. Some on this one from plaster—"

"On the other," Sunset cut in grimly, "from the bone of a woman's skull—"

"I'd bet five hundred dollars that these bullets came from the same gun."

The cabin became very quiet. Outside the mob had, temporarily, quieted down, and ceased to fire useless bullets into stout log walls. Doubtless, men had been sent to fetch oil and wood for the burning down of the cabin. But over the two gleaming bullets, Doc looked up into the hard eyes of Sunset McGee.

"Your bullet," he questioned, "came from the head of a murdered woman?"

"Yes, Doc. A woman named Hilda who was killed in Boston, Massachusetts, by her husband, a man named Frank Flarity. Boston Charley, the detective who is after him—"

"*Is?*" Doc questioned.

Sunset felt foolish when Doc used the present tense. He had not told the old official of the ruse that had been practised to throw the Firebank gang off guard, the substitution of another dead drummer for Boston Charley, the Nemesis of Frank Flarity. He told him now, briefly.

"So this detective is at Coogan's place with Rattlesnake Bill?" Doc asked.

"Yes."

"We must bring him here."

The mob began to howl like hungry wolves. The door trembled to a smashing attack. Doc turned and said to Jake, "Step over easy. Pull the edge of that blanket aside right easy. When I take the lamp off the table, shove your gun barrel out and let one slug off."

The moment Doc had removed the lamp from the table throwing the forward part of the cabin into darkness, Jake quietly pulled aside the blanket. Outside bullets had shattered a window pane. He poked the Sharps barrel out at an angle. "Now," ordered Doc.

The big gun roared. Jake's shoulder jerked to the kick. Outside the doorway sounded a sudden choking shriek, then a scurrying of feet as men dropped the battering ram and ran for their lives. Jack turned, withdrew the gun barrel, did up the blanket, spat calmly. "Downed one," he drawled.

Doc replaced the lamp. He returned to Sunset and the question of bullets. "This camp," he said "can't stand to have a woman killer running loose. First thing you know, we'd have no reputation at all. So—we bring this legal Boston detective here to lay down the law to the boys and round up this Firebank a whole lot for killing his wife."

"*Firebank?*"

"Sure." Doc touched the bullet from the wall with his forefinger. "Fred Firebank fired that one just now. Said so himself. This other was fired by Flarity. Into Hilda's head. They come from same gun. Firebank carries it now. So—unless he can talk mighty fast—he is *also Frank Flarity*."

CHAPTER XVI

So, ACCORDING TO DOC, A SHREWD AND ruthless killer tonight ruled the roost in Buckskin. He had assembled his gang after his flight from the east, set up his kingdom of rule or ruin backed by the guns of his followers like Budge, and the rest. The two slugs, according to Doc, would be enough to prove that Firebank now owned the pistol which had killed the Boston woman. But of what avail now was that knowledge with the gang surrounding Doc's cabin and on the verge of killing off all available limbs of the law in the town?

Doc locked the two murder bullets in his little black grip along with other small articles of his trade that he had hastily collected. He wasted no more talk explaining his further intentions. He said over his shoulder to old Jake, "Keep the lamp in here turned low. Don't waste no lead but snap a shot at 'em if they git too bold."

Then Doc motioned to a doorway leading into the rear of the cabin and said to Sunset, "You come with me."

The doorway gave entrance to the small room where Doc cooked. Sunset saw another doorway in the rear wall of the kitchen by the light of the lantern which Doc had lit and was carrying.

Doc ambled to this rear door, pulled it open. The bold move alarmed Sunset for he thought the official intended to step from the security of the cabin out into the open under the watchful stars.

But Doc held high the lantern and turned with a grin to the young deputy. The yellow lantern glow revealed a shadowy cave-like space adjoining the kitchen.

"Come on," Doc bade, and stepped into the cave.

Sunset, following, felt himself entering a place filled with cooler air than that in the cabin.

"You may have noticed when you came into town," Doc said, holding high his lantern, "that the cabins on my side of the street are backed up against a low ridge. Here was where the original camp was situated. And for a good reason. First we dug into the side of the hill, made dugouts and lived in 'em. Then later when we got more prosperous we built four-square cabins in front but hooked the rear of the cabins to our dugouts. There's a good reason for this." He moved the lantern back and forth slowly. Its gleam picked up the fronts of wooden bins. "We're fixed up to store our spuds and onions and other vegetables here," Doc explained. "Lots cooler in here."

He moved deeper into the dugout followed by Sunset. He halted beside a long wide wooden table. On it reposed two objects covered with canvas tarps. "I must also add," Doc said grimly, "that in my official trade, my dugout comes in handy as a cool place not only to hang up meat, but to lay out poor devils like Happy Jack and that drummer until they can be decently buried."

Sunset stepped nearer. He felt the hair bristling on the back of his neck as he sighteed, by the lantern's glow, two pairs of feet, pathetically bare, protruding from under the tarps. Here then lay the bodies of men who had fallen to the ruthless guns of Firebank and his gang.

Sunset gazed and heard himself saying grimly, "A sight, Doc, to break a decent man's heart. But here we be. In your dugout—but seems this is the end. Just the door leading into your kitchen."

"I use this place also to store spare tools and such that might clutter up the cabin," Doc advised. "Over in that corner you'll see a couple of shovels and picks. We look around and we'll find a hammer or so. Also," he grinned, "there's a ten pound metal keg of black powder and box of fuse. Worst comes to worst, that powder might come in handy."

Sunset nodded. "We could maybe stick a length of fuse in the powder keg, tamp it in tight with dirt from this cellar. Maybe open the front door of the cabin and roll it out with the fuse lit. It would cause a little temporary excitement—"

"Don't get discouraged easy, boy. Bring over a pick and shovel. Then I'll help you shove some boxes under this ventilator here."

The ventilator was a square wooden box which protruded above the dirt roof of the dugout like a chimney. It was placed there to permit the entrance of fresh air into the cave. But it was not wide enough for Slim Sunset or stocky Doc to crawl through.

"The dugout roof," said Doc, "is made of a layer of dirt about a foot thick on top. Then comes some loose brush laid on pine poles reaching from the centre pole of the dugout and slantin' down on both sides to form the roof. The idea I got in mind is for us to dig where the ventilator comes through. Widen the hole where it enters. Make the hole big enough for us to crawl up."

"But once we widen this ventilator hole in the roof," said Sunset, "and come out in the open on the dugout roof, somebody'll see us sure. We won't have a Chinaman's chance."

Doc nodded but said grimly, "We won't have that much chance if we stay in the cabin. They may have some trouble settin' it afire. But they use enough coal oil and stuff and it's bound to catch fire. I'd ruther take a gamble on prairie doggin' my way out through the ventilator hole than hangin' around to be a nice prime roast of meat for Freddy Firebank."

Sunset nodded. Wasting no more time, he fashioned a working platform under the end of the ventilator with stout wooden packing cases. He studied the job, then reached for the pick-axe. He was sore and tired, it seemed, in every muscle but this tiresome job was necessary if he hoped to get away alive.

The job proved slow and painful to muscles. Sunset was forced to stand up near the dugout ceiling. He could not take good hefty swings with the pick at the dirt and other packing around the end of the ventilator because of limited space.

But Sunset persisted. He widened the space around the ventilator's wooden end. Doc stood by encouragingly, holding the lantern so that its light would aid the deputy. Sunset's neck began to feel stiff for he was forced to cock back his head as he worked on and on for what seemed hours. Occasionally he paused for breath and wiped the sweat off his face. Doc claimed it was a cool place for vegetables or dead men. But Sunset discovered that hard arm work easily worked up a sweat. When he had widened the space around the ventilator with pick-axe and shovel, he asked Doc to hunt up other tools, particularly a hammer and a saw.

Doc put down the lantern and searched the corners

of the cellar where implements were stored. He passed up to Sunset a fairly good hammer but the saw was one fashioned to cut meat. Sunset shivered, feeling the blade with a finger. Maybe Doc used it for other cold meat besides the carcasses of deer and elk.

Dismissing that ghastly thought inspired by the sheeted bodies of Happy Jack and the drummer, Sunset now began carefully cutting through the brush and poles around the ventilator's square wooden shaft. Clods of dirt rattled down on his packing box platform, louder and louder. Once Doc cautioned him to work more quietly.

"I'm figurin'," the old man said, "that since there's no rear entrance to the cabin nor window, they won't be payin' much attention to the back. They'll be strung out in shadows around the sides and in front. But might happen that some prowler would climb over the dugout roof and hear you rattlin' away at the ventilator."

So, because Firebank's mobsters might close off this sole escape route, Sunset forced himself to work at an easier pace. But now he was alive with the bitter desire to get into the open, face the enemy, go down with blazing guns if things worked out in that fashion. But at least get out, not roast here like a rat caught in a barn fire. Despite the aches in neck, back and arm muscles, he wished to push himself to the very limit of his endurance. But he was forced by Doc's advice to go cautiously and—above all—patiently.

Then came the time when he felt the ventilator move loosely as he grasped its lower edges. He knew then that one good pull would drag it down into the cellar leaving a hole up through the dirt roof large enough for men to push their bodies. An aperture that he had dug even to accommodate Doc's portly form. It seemed to Sunset that hours had elapsed, that when they emerged, coming daylight would reveal their bodies outlined on the dugout's roof above the town's main street. He said as much to Doc. But the old man chuckled. "A long time to go before crack of day. How big you got that hole? Big enough for me and Jake?"

"I'm sure of that."

Doc laughed grimly. "Then," he said, "it's wide enough for us to pass up this little ten pound keg of black powder. You stay there on guard. I'll go and fetch Jake. We'll stick a short length of fuse in the head of the powder keg, pack it down with mud. When we get out—"

Before Sunset could ask further questions, Doc set down the lantern. He left the dim dugout to call Jake while Sunset waited in the half darkness with two dead men for company.

The three men moved swiftly after Doc had returned with Jake. Experienced in powder work, they tamped the short length of fuse into the head of the powder keg, converting the keg into a rude homemade bomb.

Then Doc gave the orders. "Sunset'll go first. Jake second. Then Jake'll reach down the hole and grab the powder keg. Now if nobody spots you two, lay as low as you can, until I can get up on top with you. After that—'

Sunset forced his body up through the widened ventilator shaft first, feeling dirt and dust rain down on his head and inside the neck of his shirt. He emerged on hands and knees on the dugout roof. He had holstered his guns but nobody was there to dispute his breakout.

For a moment he lay flat on his stomach, filling his lungs with the sweet night air of the mountain country. From his position he could look down into the brightly lighted main street of the town. They had built a large bonfire some distance to the front.

Sunset marked the forms of members of the mob clustered carelessly around the bonfire. He believed that he saw Fred Firebank moving about in command. But he could not waste time making sure of the gang leader. He put his face to the dark maw of the ventilator shaft and whispered hoarsely. "All quiet. Come on, Jake. I'll reach down and help you by taking your hands."

"First," Jake said, "grab this old rifle and bag of spare shells." And he thrust the Sharps buffalo gun up through the shaft. And after it, a dozen finger-length fifty calibre shells stored in a small buckskin bag. Then, aided by Sunset, the driver worked his way up and out on the roof.

"All quiet in Buckskin," whispered Sunset as they lay resting and regaining their wind.

Jake clicked a cartridge into the breech of the Sharps and said longingly, "Boy—wouldn't I like to bust one round down into that bonfire. Wouldn't those hellions run for sour apples?"

"No shootin' yet," warned Sunset. "We must trust now to Doc. He seems to pack all the horse-sense in this outfit tonight."

Assured that they had not been seen crouching on the dark roof, the two then brought up the keg of powder. After that, they aided Doc to puff his way up the shaft and out under the starlight.

"Once," Doc panted, "when I was younger and slimmer I had to dig my way out of a cabin which was rimmed in by hostile Injuns. Never figgered I'd have to repeat. Wait a minute, boys, until I git my breath and my old heart quits hammerin'. Then we'll make out next move."

The dugout roof smoothly joined that of the cabin in front. There was no saddle permitted in which snow water or rain could settle and work its way down through the ceiling.

"This powder keg," said Doc, "won't do much but cause a little excitement. But that's all we need."

CHAPTER XVII

Doc THEN HURRIEDLY ISSUED FINAL INstructions. They would tote the powder keg to the end of the cabin roof overlooking the main street. Choosing the right moment, they would light the end of the fuse and drop the keg down from the roof into the main street.

"It's round. Likely it'll roll some," judged Doc. "Only chance we take is that the fuse'll go out."

"It's cut short," Jake said grimly, "and we'll take pains to put on a danged good light. That's my job."

"Mine," said Sunset.

All three knew that the man who struck and held the match might easily be revealed as a target to some sure marksman in the street.

Doc had to chuckle. "You two can fight it out between you. But the minute you drop the keg, turn around and scamper like scairt coyotes back along this roof. We'll head up this hill in back. There's some brush up there for cover. If we get there without bein' hurt, we can catch our wind and figure what comes next."

Sunset said grimly, "I want to find a horse so I can ride out and get help at Happy Jack's place from Boston Charley and Rattlesnake Bill."

"There's a barn down back of Firebank's hotel," said Doc. "Maybe there's some saddle ponies in the corral. We'll try that if we ever live to climb the hill."

When Doc gave the word, Sunset and Jake crawled toward the front end of the dirt roof, rolling the powder keg ahead as they advanced. They took their time, fearful that some street scout might spot them. But the glare of the huge bonfire helped them. Also, the eyes of the crowd were now centred on six men who were advancing cautiously for another attack on the front door of the cabin.

Flattened out on the cabin roof, peering down into the street, Sunset said to Jake, "There's Firebank over there giving orders."

Clearly they heard Firebank's sharp commands to his men. He was bidding them smash down the cabin door with the pine corral pole which they were using as a battering ram.

One of the battering ram party objected in a surly way. "That old driver might pump a buffaler slug into one of us we get too frisky."

Firebank laughed disagreeably. "In this world we all got to run chances. Go ahead and smash in that door. We've waited long enough."

But Sunset noted that Firebank made no move to come near the cabin. Fearless Fred had stationed himself across the street by the fire. Urged on then by their chief's orders, the six men advanced slowly. They trotted across the street with the long pole balanced between them. There were three men grasping the pole on each side.

Whong. The first punch against the cabin door was a lukewarm effort. The moment the battering ram struck, the six men cast themselves down into the street dirt. They did this to escape any whistling slug that old Jake might fire their way through the front window of the cabin.

Firebank cursed them into renewed action. He pointed out that Jake had not fired on them. "Maybe," he encouraged, "the old fool has run out of shells."

In this second attack the six men seized the pole with greater courage. They smashed its end against the cabin door. Sunset, flattened out on the dirt roof, felt it shake beneath him.

"*Again!*" yelled Firebank. And, excitedly, the leader stepped away from the fire and into the street.

The six men came trotting forward.

Sunset heard old Doc's low call. "Any time now, boys. Touch her off!"

Sunset stirred, began to reach for a match in his overalls pocket. He heard old Jake's urgent order: "You be ready to roll the powder keg off the roof. I got me a match ready." An interval with both men breathing hard as race horses after a tight finish. Then the match flared. Sparks flew from the end of the short length of fuse.

"*Let 'er go!*" yelled Jake. And at that shout, Sunset put his hands against the keg and thrust it forward with all his might.

Some member of the mob arrayed by the bonfire spotted the flicker of light as Jake scratched the match. "Look out!" the scout roared. "Look out on the cabin roof!"

Every eye turned toward the roof. Not a man in that whisky-brave mob but now saw the sputtering red sparks and understood where they came from. Many there were prospectors and used powder to work their claims every day of the week.

Jake arose and yelped boldly. "Look out below! *Black powder!*" But that warning was not necessary.

As the keg plunged from the roof with sparks from the length of fuse flashing in the dark night, every member of the mob stampeded. Even Firebank turned and ran like a scared wolf.

The six men at the front door dropped their battering ram pole. They turned in blind panic and bunched up as they ran across the wide street. The round keg hit the ground just in front of the yielding cabin door. There was a slight downward slope from the cabin toward the bonfire. The moment that the keg hit the earth it began to roll.

It seemed to be pursuing the six men who had worked with the battering ram. One man, as he galloped from danger, looked over his shoulder and bellowed to his mates. "The danged thing's chasin' us! Boys—*run for your lives!*"

If Sunset and Jake had died the next moment, they would have hesitated there to laugh at the retreat of the mob and the battering ram party. Only the sharp yell of old Doc, accentuated by the roar of the buffalo gun, recalled them to the peril still remaining of escaping to the brush on the crest of the ridge.

"You boxheads!" Doc brawled. "Come on! Do you figger this is a Punch and Judy show?"

Halfway across the wide street, not ten feet from the heels of the last fugitive of the battering ram gang, the powder keg hit a rock and a rut that stayed its progress. It held up for the split part of a second. Then the fire on the short cut fuse burned down into the black powder. *Wham!*

As Sunset attempted to regain his feet, the shock wave from the powder blast shook the cabin. He fell flat on his stomach and shielded his head with his arms. His ear drums reverberated to the rumbling roar. He believed that the next moment would be his last, that some exploded fragment of the town of Buckskin would come flying through the air and brain him. He felt the trembling and jiggling of the dirt roof beneath his body.

He wanted to raise his head and retch and empty his stomach. The sharp and nauseating odour of burnt black powder sickened him.

But after what was but a moment but seemed an eternity, the shivering of the roof ended. Sunset raised up cautiously on his elbows. To his ears came a confused sound like the bawling of cattle. His eyes were blinded by the red glare of light which had flashed when the powder keg blew up. Finally he recognized the confusion of sound that beat against his ears as the doleful and panicky yelling of the Buckskinners.

Then a huge rude hand grasped Sunset by the shoulder and he heard the breathless command of Jake: "Let's git outa here!"

Staggering up, never waiting to look down into the main street, the two lunged back along the roof until Doc's sharp authoritative voice checked them. "You boxheads," he rapped out, "are plungin' around like you got the blind staggers. You shoulda had sense enough to blind your eyes when that powder keg let go."

On the hard man-killing climb up the side of the ridge into which Buckskin's pioneers had carved their dugouts, Doc acted as guide. When the three paused halfway up toward sheltering brush, he told them that he had turned his back and thus protected his vision when he saw Jake scratch his match.

"You two ranihans," he scolded, "mighta come outa this in bad shape as though you were snowblind. That there blast mighta seared your eyeballs."

In the few moments required to follow Doc up the hill, the mists cleared partially from the sight of the two powder keg monkeys. The velvety darkness of the western night was also like a caress to eyes before which a red ball of fire seemed to dance and glitter. When they reached a mossy down log on the edge of a scraggy line of limber pine, they cast themselves down behind it, gulped in fresh air, and, for the first time since the explosion, looked down into the town of Buckskin.

The sight amazed Sunset. He gasped and stammered to Doc, "Gee whillikens! We set the danged burg on fire!"

Buckskin was a ramshackle burg, its main street lined on both sides with a variety of plank and log buildings and also many tents. The summer had been a dry one. A good stiff breeze was blowing up the valley. The wind was wafting blazing embers through the black night. Sunset saw these firebrands sparkle redly as they were picked up, swooped into the sky, then pulled down by gravity to settle on the roofs of tents and buildings.

The fire did not catch where cabins had dirt roofs. But when sparks and bits of burning material settled on the tops of dingy canvas tents, the tent blazed up and into smoking black ruin in a moment.

Here and there, too, were pine trees which had not been cut out when the hasty miners got ready to root for gold and had no time for civic improvement. Many of these pines were dying from the top down. When fire struck half dead trees, they exploded like Roman candles shooting more sparks and flaming branches through the air.

"And to think," Sunset marvelled, "it all was caused by one little old teeny keg of powder."

He couldn't understand how that small amount of explosive would so quickly cause this terrifying and bullet-swift sweep of the fire. He had counted on the explosion frightening the mobsters and temporarily diverting their attention thus allowing himself and Doc and Jake time to escape. But he certainly had never foreseen that ten pounds of powder would possess this power of merciless destruction.

Doc explained it. "They had built that big bonfire," he said, "just across the street from my cabin. The next move would be to try and set fire to the cabin. So they had likely brought down stuff that would burn easy like dry hay and pitch pine. And probably soaked the stuff in kerosene. Once they got that door battered down and us cornered back in the rear, they'd pile all this stuff up along the walls and set it on fire. Then when we come scootin' out with our shirt tails blazin', they'd laugh and shoot us down. That is—if they didn't grab one of us for a public hanging. As it was—"

Doc sighed gustily. "As it was," he said softly, "the blast of the powder blew the bonfire to blazin' bits. Sparks and stuff landed on the oil-soaked wood and hay. The wind picked up the blazin' bits and began blowin' them up the street. When fire touched a tent, the tent whooped up in a hurry. It was like pushin' over a line of dominoes. Shove the first one, and the others all keel over."

Then Jake spoke solemnly in the gloom, gazing down at the fire-riddled town. "So it'll be with Buckskin!"

"So it'll be with Buckskin," sighed Doc. He paused a moment. Then he went on. "But I remember I helped to start this burg. I—I hate to see her burn for after all, Buckskin was my home town."

But Sunset, with the ruthlessness of youth, growled, "It *was* your home town, Doc, until the Firebank gang turned up and took over. Then it was *their* town."

"Yeah," said Doc. "Yeah—I guess you're right. Well —if you fellows can see let's pull our freight."

CHAPTER XVIII

Now THAT HIS VISION HAD CLEARED UP, SUNSET took the lead in the slow jog up the ridge. He was thinking of the stable in the rear of the hotel. He thought he might be able to pick up a saddle horse there. He knew now that he required help and the nearest must come from Happy Jack's road ranch. There was also a barn in the rear of the stage office where a fourup of stage horses was stabled to serve on the run from Buckskin out to Happy Jack's.

Sunset believed he was setting a good stiff pace toward a point on the ridge from which he could climb down to the rear of the hotel. But as he scrambled over the rough ground, an occasional glance down into the smoky valley indicated that the fire was running up the main street faster than a man could trot.

The three had almost reached the point on the ridge above hotel and stage office when they halted at the sound of hoofs booming on the earth and the loud nickerings of panic-stricken horses. Straight across their front charged the animals, sharply outlined against the red glare of the blazing town, manes and tails streaming in the wind. The ponies whipped over the top of the crest, then galloped crashingly into the thin timber and away from hell's fire and smoke.

"There goes your horses," said Jake. "Somebody had brains enough to let 'em outa barns and corrals so they wouldn't burn up."

And there also went Sunset's present hope of getting a mount for the dash to Happy Jack's for help.

Doc had swung around, squinted his eyes against the red flaring lights and was estimating the situation. All he owned in the world including his possession under the law of the corpses of Happy Jack and the drummer was now in danger of destruction. Only the width of the main street at present was saving Doc's place and other buildings on its side of the street.

Doc laughed grimly and held up his little black bag. "All I got for a new start in life," he commented. That was all. No tears for Buckskin from him.

Jake shrugged. "That's more than I got," he growled. "And if that wind throws the fire across the street I'll be out of my driving job."

Sunset cut in, trying to cheer up the old fellows. "Well," he said, "we're at least out here in the open. Not cornered in a blazing cabin."

"We're out here," said Doc, "but we still got to get out of this town."

"If them Buckskinners ever lay hands on us," Jake added, "they'll skin us alive."

Sunset nodded. This was no time to preach a sermon, point out that if Buckskinners hadn't been so greedy they could have guarded their town from a gang, all this would not have happened. Buckskin was burning because it had been turned over, lock, stock, and barrel, to a ruthless lawless gang. It had been Buckskin or bust. Now the town would need another war cry.

That cry came on the instant, shrilling up from below, originating in a knot of men who were scurrying around like black ants repairing a damaged hill. Some of these citizens were running in and out of the bar room of the hotel. Some, emerging, were laden with cases. Others trundled barrels. The destruction of Buckskin was greeted with the bellow, "Let 'er burn but save the whisky!"

All that perilous flaming smoky night, that shout re-echoed along the street.

"Let 'er burn but save the whisky!"

Some of Firebank's men were there carrying liquor from the hotel before the wind flung flames across the street against the tinder-dry front of the two-storey building.

There was nothing in Buckskin with which to fight fire, not even a hose-cart hauled by volunteers. So, in the fashion of many frontier towns that had burned before this and would burn after, bucket brigades were organized. Blazing tents were hauled down and the flames beaten out. But always there sounded the angry hiss and crackling of the red fire sweeping up the valley.

Then, suddenly, Sunset felt against his face the sudden cut of a brisk breeze. And just as suddenly his nostrils and throat were choked by greasy smoke. He heard the loud alarmed yell of old Jake. "Wind's shifted our way!"

That would throw flaming embers across the street. Sunset remembered that he had left two women and Lonesome Luke at bay down in that threatened hotel. He had been warned by Jake that all the Buckskinners would blame the three men in the cabin for setting their town on fire, that they would seek bloody revenge if they caught up with the fugitives.

"I'm goin' down there," Sunset said desperately. "I can't stay up here, safe. Those two women."

As he turned to run down the hill, Jake seized his shoulders and tried to wrestle him to the earth. "Stay here, you fool!" bawled Jake. "If them females got the sense Gawd give 'em, they've run out of the hotel by now."

But Sunset resisted Jake mightily. He was remembering a pretty lady law who had scorned him. He was thinking about the weeping sister from Boston of a murdered woman. His mind was on a lanky grey outlaw gambler who had thrown in this lot with an outmatched law dog because that outlaw had fallen in love with a timid school teacher.

Doc intervened. "If one of us goes down," he said, "we might as well *all go*. But let's use some sense about this thing."

Then the wise old man pointed out that the soot and smoke of the fire would plaster their features with grime until they would be unrecognizable. "But me," groaned Doc, "I got to be extra careful because no smoke will ever disguise my shape."

Doc's cool common sense restrained Sunset's youthful desire to enter into the burning town and discover what had happened to the women. Therefore he took his time clambering down the side of the steep ridge. Leading Jake and Doc, he came finally to Buckskin Creek winding along through its brushy course. There was barely enough water in the little stream to provide Buckskin with drinking and washing water. Sunset recalled that when the retreat was made from Doc's dugout, the three fugitives had crossed Buckskin on a foot log.

Hidden in the brush, the three friends paused to reconnoitre before they forded the creek and entered the smoky blazing camp. As they crouched in the willows, they heard the confused bawling of the panic-stricken firefighters in the town, now and then rising like the humming of swarming bees above the crackling noise of the great fire.

The rears of the buildings along the main street stood out blackly against the red flaring light. The awkward outline of the hotel could easily be made out. And near it the squat adobe building that housed the stage office. Sunset recalled now, how he had once decided in his anger to go there and wire in his resignation to the Piute sheriff. This moment, that time seemed years in the past. But only a few hours had passed.

Sunset turned and said to Doc, "There's a chance if we can get into the stage office of wiring Piute to send help."

"If the wire ain't down, I'd say that wire has already been sent."

Now, through an opening between stage office and hotel, Sunset squinted his eyes at sight of a team of horses passing down main street on the run. And he heard again the distant wail: "Let 'er burn and save the whisky."

He turned to Doc with a sneer, nodding toward the laden wagon which the team drew. "I suppose there goes some of Firebank's liquid wealth."

But Doc shook his head. "I'd sooner reckon they are fetching barrels of water from up the creek for the bucket brigades. Ain't enough water here in the creek to do much good. Too low."

"Queer," commented Sunset, "that Buckskin Creek would be so low early in the summer."

"Not strange around a mining camp like this one. Most of the claims are placers. Takes plenty of water to do placer minin'. The gold is washed out of the dirt, you know. Not like a gold mine where they blast the ore from rock."

"Yeah. But this creek usually runs quite a good head of water."

Doc shrugged. "Well, these gold crazy fools in camp went up above town about a mile. Above the real rich placer ground. They diverted the most of the creek water from the main course into a good-sized reservoir. Dammed up a gulch to hold it. Then they would have plenty of reserve water to wash out gold even though in town we might go short for drinking."

Jake cut in, "And for fires like this one."

"I reckon," Doc ended casually, "they are now haulin' water in barrels from that reservoir."

"Barrels and barrels," said Sunset, studying the wall of fire which now was shooting flames high into the air, "will never stop this one." He arose and stretched his legs. He was tired and sore but in the face of this blistering emergency, he had drawn on his reserves. He knew that he now could stay on his feet until he ascertained the fate of Dulcy and Mildred.

He waded across the little stream. The water didn't reach his knees. He heard Jake splash after him. He waited for them before he climbed the opposite bank which would bring the three nearer the town and its mob of excited firefighters.

"Maybe we can get into the stage office first," he suggested. "See if the wire's still workin'. Send a report on all this to sheriff."

Jake and Doc didn't object. Silently they crawled up from the creek, worked their way slowly through the darkness toward the rear of the adobe office. They passed the hay yard and barn where stage teams were stabled and paused briefly to check on the horses. Jake, lover of good horses, was particularly concerned. They found not a horse in the stalls.

"I'm glad," Jake said, greatly relieved. "Likely there was stage horses in that bunch we saw runnin' over the ridge. Agent probably turned 'em loose so they wouldn't burn up."

They reached the rear door of the doby building. One dirty rear window showed a dim yellow glow but Sunset didn't know whether the light came from an inside light or was the reflection of dancing flames across the street in front of the place.

"Next job is to get in," he said.

Jake solved that instantly. As driver, he carried a key to the rear door with him. He cautiously opened the door but warned his friends. "Go in slow. Have guns ready. Somebody might be on guard over the safe."

Jake proved a prophet. The three filed through a room dimly lit by a lantern which served as a storage room. Jake turned the knob of the door that gave entrance to the office. The moment he pulled open the door, a sharp order rang out. "Put up your hands!" and then, "Who are you?"

Sunset recognized the voice of the stage line agent and heard Jake's sigh of relief. The old driver whispered, "It's me and Doc and the law from Piute."

"Come in," said the agent.

He had a lantern lit and sitting on the floor. He was emptying the stage line safe. "This doby won't burn easy," he said, "but I'm gettin' out of here."

"How about your wire?" suggested Sunset. "Can we get through to Piute for help?"

The agent cursed bitterly. "Firebank and his fools cut the wire just before they organized up to burn out you and Doc and Jake."

CHAPTER XIX

THAT, THOUGHT SUNSET, SETTLED THE HASH for Buckskin. Then the agent spoke again. "But earlier tonight I took it on myself to wire Piute that things were boiling over." He was crouching in front of the safe looking up at Sunset. "Of course I did it without your authority."

"You showed some sense at that. More than I did."

"Then," the agent went on, "after that fight you had with Budge and his gang over the Chinaman," he frowned, "I think he said his name was Yum and he had cooked for my friend, Happy Jack. This Yum came to me for help."

"Help?"

"Yeah. He asked for the loan of a saddle pony. Knowin' a Chinaman wasn't much of a rider, I hesitated some. But he dug up good money and laid it down for rent on the pony. A hundred dollars. I got it here in the safe. Well, I furnished him with what I consider a good safe pony and he took off with his shirt tail fluttering in the wind."

The agent scratched his lean jaw, thinking deeply. "He said if Sunset McGee came along later, to tell him he was ridin' to warn the fat man who sells Painkiller. I didn't understand his jargon but I'm just passing it along."

Now Sunset at last understood the part the wily Chinese had played. He had wormed himself into the confidence of the gang by fawning on Firebank. But when peril struck, he had carried out Sunset's earlier rather hastily issued order to warn Boston Charley and Rattlesnake Bill to come to Buckskin if needed. Certainly they were needed now. Although two men, however brave, could do little against the angry Buckskinners.

While Sunset and the agent talked, Doc roved around the office. He was studying its contents. The agent had stacked up more than valuables for removal from the adobe in case the fire threatened to catch and burn down the place.

Doc waddled back into the ring of light cast by the agent's lantern.

"You know I started this fire with a little old keg of blastin' powder," he drawled.

The agent nodded. And commented dryly. "We all know it. A lot of them yellin' hyenas out there will rack your neck if they lay hands on you."

Doc rubbed his chin. "This was a good little old camp," he went on, "before the boys got the get-rich-quick bug. Powder started her to burnin'. And maybe powder can help to save her."

"Firebank's bunch are yelling to let the camp burn and save all the whisky."

" I heard 'em. Kegs of whisky represent real wealth to them rats so far from the railroad. But I just saw that you had some spare kegs of powder stacked up over there."

"Yeah. Some we hauled in on order. About six kegs. Miner who ordered it, never got around to taking it away. The stuff's dangerous so I figure to roll it out in back and dump it in the creek before the fire gets across the street."

Doc turned to Jake. "Now if we had a wagon and some horses—"

Jake frowned. "What's on your mind?"

"I'm thinkin' of that reservoir above town. If we could get up there with this powder and blow out the headgate, a wall of water would come sweepin' down here."

"It would make quite a flood," said the agent.

Doc shrugged and jerked a thumb toward the dancing red reflections in the front windows that came from flames just across the street. "Which would you ruther have," he asked, "mud in here to clean out? Or a heap of ashes to rebuild on?"

The agent scratched his head. "Well—I guess I'd prefer mud. That can be cleaned out."

"But where can we find horses?" pondered Jake. "The agent here run off all the horses, for which I thank him."

"Not all," said the agent. "Firebank's gang came along and requisitioned a stage coach and one of your wheel teams. They drove it up to the theatre to load up the whisky stored there and haul it away."

Jake began to curse. He growled that it was a dastardly shame that a good wheel team and coach should be used to save whisky while a town was burning down.

Doc narrowed his eyes at his companions "If we could somehow cut out that coach and team, load this powder on it, and have Jake to drive to the reservoir dam, we might do some good for this camp."

The agent shook his head. "There's a dozen Firebank's men up there on guard or loadin' the liquor."

Doc glanced at Jake who nodded slowly. "I'm with you," said Jake, "if I can borrow a riot gun here from the agent."

"Take your pick. There's a sawed-off ten-gauge

Greener over there in the case. And plenty reloads."

"Me," said Doc, as Jake went to fetch the shotgun, "I am packin' a buffalo gun." He glanced at Sunset. But the latter frowned.

"I am more concerned with what happened to Lonesome Luke and the two women," said Sunset, "than in saving this camp. I'd like to search the hotel before it catches afire."

"You may run into some of that bunch," remonstrated the agent. "They took Budge in there after you nigh killed him."

Sunset wasn't listening. The time was past for fear. He was watching old Doc. Finally he spoke his wonder. "Earlier you were ready to run away and let Firebank take over your town. Now you'd risk your neck to save the danged place." Sunset shook his red head in honest bewilderment.

Doc listened with a smile on his face. He nodded. "I agree with you," he answered. "I really this minute don't understand myself. Yeah—once life seemed sweeter to me than facin' up to the gang. But now—when I see the town on fire, the camp that me and my long gone friends started and was so proud of—" His head dropped. Only for a moment. Then the old man was himself again; cool, proud of eye, ever alert for the main chance.

His tough spirit took hold of Jake. "I'm not much on brains," the driver declared. "All I know what to do good is drive horses. You name the game, Doc. And I'll sit in with you to the last call."

Doc faced the agent. "I'm burned out," he said. "All I own is this little black bag and maybe the dugout behind my shack and what's in it. To wit: two dead men, that school teacher's trunk, a couple

BUCKSKIN RIDER 171

bins of spuds and onions. But if you'll stand good for me, I'll buy those six kegs of powder."

The agent shrugged and grinned. "Your credit is always good with me, Doc. If you can get a team to haul that stuff, I'll help you load and touch her off!"

Thus, hastily, in the doby was framed the forlorn hope of saving Buckskin from fiery destruction. Because two old men mourned that once it had been a good camp.

"As for you, son," Doc said to Sunset. "Go ahead and hunt for your sweetheart."

"Not my sweetheart. Just a girl."

"Just a girl, son. But you are young and I am old and once I, too, had a bonny, bonny girl. So—forget me and the camp and *go for her*."

Leaving the agent on guard over his safe and powder kegs, the three crept up the dark alley. Jake and Doc planned to scout out the loading procedure in front of the theatre. Sunset hoped to work his way into the hotel through the rear.

"Best way," whispered Doc, "is to sneak in through the kitchen. They'll all mostly be out in front fightin' the fire."

But Sunset shook his head. He stepped up on the wooden stairway which led to the second floor. He had descended these steps after his final encounter with Dulcy. He recalled that bitter flight now with remorse. He hadn't given the girl the least credit of doubt. She had said that appearances were against her and he had been picked up in a sudden fit of insane jealousy. Standing here, staring up the dark flight of steps, he thought of what Doc had said, that Dulcy Pringle was his sweetheart. Not until this moment when he more than half believed he had lost her forever did he finally acknowledge that he loved her.

Jake brought him back to reality by a warning touch on his arm. "There's men on the roof," he whispered. "Probably up there throwin' buckets of water around and beating out sparks that light. Be careful of them. Take plenty of time and don't get your head shot off."

Sunset said in farewell—for he thought that he stood a good chance of never seeing his two friends alive again. "If I can make it, I'll get there to help you with the horses."

"Don't worry about us," Doc said in parting. "Take care of the women."

"Women and children first," old Jake agreed as he turned and trotted into the darkness hot on the heels of Doc.

Sunset tiptoed up the dark enclosed stairway, gun held ready for action at close quarters. None disputed him. When he paused to listen, he heard now the shouts above and the thud of boots of men working desperately on the hotel roof to save the building.

The door that gave entrance to the second floor stood agape. Bitter smoke trailed from it and almost made Sunset choke and cough. But keeping his silence, he stepped cautiously into the long hallway. It was dim but the feeble light of a turned-down oil lamp in its bracket on the wall half way along the gloomy corridor.

As he moved along, he came first to Firebank's room, tried the door, discovered that now it had been locked. He went on toward the doorway of the women's room. He was halfway down the hall, standing directly under the lamp when he heard loud steps on the flight of stairs that led up from the lobby.

"I'll root 'em out," a man snarled.

Sunset dropped flat on his stomach on the floor as he saw Slim Osage step into sight from the lobby stairway. Slim didn't look down the hall but turned to the door of the women's room. He began to batter it with his fist, bawling loudly for those inside to open up, that the play was all over. A woman inside began a shrill screaming. Slim Osage laughed roughly. He turned and called down the stairway, "Come on up, boys!"

Two members of the gang came into sight crowding closely after Slim. They joined in his laughter. Slim called a second time to the shrieking woman. "Your gamblin' man is dead and gone. We just shot him!"

Then a lean grey man came into sight staggering up into the hallway from the lobby. His face looked bloodless. His lips were pressed tightly together. Blood dripped from his trailing right arm. It was Lonesome Luke.

"Wrong, Slim," Luke whispered between those dry taut lips. And he raised his gun with his left hand and began to shoot. Slim Osage turned, went down, with a bullet choking off the laugh in his mouth. His two aides whirled to bend guns on Luke. The latter was breaking at the knees.

Sunset McGee sprang to his feet. "This way, boys!" he yelled.

They turned, snarling like wolves, to face him. Thus they were caught, cut down instantly by the crossfire between Sunset and Luke.

CHAPTER XX

It was Sunset who first jumped over the writhing bodies piled up in the hall, briefly noting as he did so the glint of cuffs still embracing the hairy wrists of Slim. Luke was down on his knees with the strength draining redly from his right arm. The face he turned up to the deputy appeared to be covered now with cold wet clay. Then Sunset knowing that time was short—for the volleying gunfire would have been heard below—pounded on the door and shouted the name of Miss Mildred and gave his own. When she did not instantly open, Lonsome Luke feebly added his entreaty: "Honey—they didn't get me yet."

Then Mildred opened the door and when she saw the tall grey man kneeling and threatening to fall over, she ran to him and held him in her arms. "Oh," she cried. "You're hurt. That blood—" and instantly raising her skirt, she tore off the hem, and began fashioning it into a tourniquet to stop the flow of blood from her swain's arm.

"We must get out of here!" Sunset entreated. "Listen! You can hear men down in the lobby!"

Mildred knelt by her lover. She defied Sunset. "Where Luke goes, I go. Where he stays—there I'll stay." And as she talked, her careful expert fingers fashioned the saving strap that staunched the flow of life from Luke.

"There's a flask in my room," cried Mildred. She flushed faintly. "Mister Luke left it for me. A sort of—of—reviver!"

BUCKSKIN RIDER 175

Sunset dashed in and out, thrust flask against the teeth of Luke. Colour flooded the grey man's clay-like face. The sweat at last stood out on his brow. "Now—if you'll help," he whispered, "I can make out to walk."

So the dauntless gunman who had risked his all for his lady love tottered down the long hallway. Sunset walked on one side. Mildred the other. Gone now her weeping and softness. She said to Luke once as they heard the crash of boots on the lobby steps, "Give me your gun, Luke. They must not take us alive!"

The gambler grinned fondly down on her despite his agony. "Honey—they won't."

Reaching the door that gave onto the outside stairway, Sunset told Mildred to guide Luke down to the alley. "I'll wait here," he said.

Luke broke in but weakly, "I'm about done for," he offered. "Let me do the waitin'."

"No," Sunset growled. "You've done enough." And then—before they left him—he asked the question he hated to ask. "What—whatever happened to Dulcy?"

Luke bowed his head and shook it sadly. "That—that's my fault. That girl wouldn't stay put. I had 'em in the room and was standin' guard. Then this Slim called from the hallway. Seemed like they suspicioned Mildred had something with her would identify the killer of her sister. A letter of something—"

"Yes," murmured Mildred. "I have a letter that my sister sent me after the wedding. In it she described her husband—how he looked. I offered to give it up if they'd let us go—Dulcy and Luke and myself. But my offer was turned down. Dulcy somehow got the door unlocked and went runnin' out swearin' she'd make Firebank tell the truth. Luke tore after her down the lobby steps. He was shouting for her to come back. But—she wouldn't."

Luke interrupted. "When I got down there they had grabbed Dulcy. I see this One-Eared Budge layin' dead on the floor where they had hauled him in from the street. Firebank was goin' out the door with Dulcy fightin' in his arms. Slim Osage turned and caught me with a slug that paralysed my gun arm. I crawled off the last step and got behind the desk. But I lost blood and I reckon," he looked shame-faced, "I reckon I passed out. Until—until I heard Mildred begin to scream. Then—then I crawled up the steps—"

Sunset said between his teeth. "Fred Firebank doesn't know it. But Doc has the deadwood on him. Doc's sure that Firebank is really Frank Flarity the man who murdered your sister." He nodded down the stairway. "Go on. I'll follow—if nobody interferes."

But if any of the gang had thought to come up the lobby stairs, the sight of the three men sprawled in front of Mildred's room made their courage lukewarm. At least they slowly scouted out their advance thus giving Sunset time to turn and follow Mildred and Luke down into the alley. Undoubtedly men marked their retreat. But once the three had reached the alley, they were protected by its darkness. The stage office was the nearest place where first aid could be given to Luke. Sunset helped Mildred guide him there. And saw that the formerly meek little teacher— now a wildcat where her true love was concerned— was given the help of the agent in binding up Luke's sorely wounded arm.

With conscience cleared, Sunset now turned in

search of the girl he loved. He didn't doubt but that Firebank had taken her to his headquarters up the street, the theatre once owned by Happy Jack. That way Doc and Jake had headed earlier in hope of somehow cutting out the team of horses and the stage coach. As Sunset slipped along the dark alley, he heard from the street, again and again, the long-drawn woeful war whoop.

"Let her burn but save the whisky!"

Before leaving the stage office, he had reloaded his Colt hand gun. But he had doubly armed himself by borrowing a thirty thirty calibre Winchester carbine and box of shells from the stage company's armament. The snub-nosed carbine would be a power of strength in any long range fight into which he blundered.

He advanced now with a fierce hope warming his heart. The girl still lived—that is she had lived until lately. She was a pretty morsel. A man like Firebank would not wipe her out so long as he could enjoy her beauty and her quickening anger. Firebank would be like a sleek cat playing with a gallant mouse. He would have his fun before he killed her as he had toyed with Hilda before he put a bullet in her head.

Slipping up the alley, Sunset paused occasionally at places where narrow openings between buildings offered a view of the main street. The general tumult had slackened. Men were not running around so wildly, shouting for help to save their shacks and tents. They had generally organised into bucket brigades and were saving lung power for the difficult job of holding a fire line down the middle of main street.

One larger opening indicated to Sunset that firefighter squads had run ahead of the leaping flames, tearing down tents and wrecking flimsy cabins thus giving the main fire nothing to feed upon. Just now, too, the prevailing wind favoured the battlers for it had veered and was not hurling flaming sparks and embers across the street to buildings like the hotel and theatre.

Even as Sunset stood watching, cloaked by inky shadows, he saw the stage coach thunder past, drawn by Jake's wheel team. Kegs of liquor had been crammed aboard the big Concord. One of Firebank's men sat high on the box, yelling to the team, and aided by a friend who sat beside him using the whip to speed on the horses. Sunset surmised the liquor would be hauled outside the fire zone, hastily rolled out. Then the coach would return for another load.

"Save the whisky!" That was the war whoop which had stung old Doc into action. In its dying moments, in the red hell into which it had been converted, Buckskin drew no regrets from the gang that had made it a mockery. They cared not one iota now for its earlier days of courage and loyalty when pioneers had dug into the hillside and starved and froze to convert Buckskin into what they called a good little old camp.

Firebank and his bunch would win here, shrug off momentary disaster, move on with their bad whisky, crooked cards, their painted vice to some other wide open careless camp where men, mad for quick wealth, didn't care how it was won.

With a load of liquor being run out of town, Sunset surmised the loading gang in the theatre would be short at least two or three men. Beyond rolling other barrels to the doorway, those around the theatre would be off guard and resting. He hadn't heard a sound—not one ripple of gunfire—to indicate that Doc and Jake had gone into action. But they must move soon for despite the gaps created along its front by torn down tents and wrecked cabins, the fire was slowly but inexorably advancing. More than half the opposite side of the street now lay in smoking blackened ruins.

Sunset reached a dark and narrow doorway jutting off the alley which formerly had been the stage entrance to the theatre. Here costumed members of whatever troupe was playing within were wont to gather and quaff drinks and enjoy cool breezes between acts. In his infrequent past trips to Buckskin, Sunset had quite often gaped at the pretty gaudily costumed chorus girls and the painted tragedians and comedians taking a moment off here. The door opened to his touch. He dared not strike a match. He almost broke a leg falling down a short flight of steps but regained his balance. He stood listening a moment fearing the crash of his clumsy boots might set up an alarm. But he heard nothing beyond the distant clamour of men fighting the fire and the hiss of flames like the distant roll of waves on the seashore.

Sunset did not count himself as familiar with the backstage rooms of a theatre. His sole experience had been gained as a member of the audience in front of the stage. But he had been in this theatre in happier times when Jack Coogan operated it. The stage was not a large one but opened upon a narrow hall where men of the camp could sit at tables, smoke, and drink and laugh and enjoy whatever acts happened to be doing a turn on the stage. Most of these acts were offered by dancers and singers for Buckskin's tastes did not run to high art. Generally some male or female singer was a steady on the payroll and there was always a busy professor pounding the tin pan piano in the pit.

Finding himself in a pit of darkness, Sunset stood listening again. Then, risking hostile guns, he struck and lit a match.

By the feeble yellow light, he looked around him. His surroundings, at first glance, where wholly strange. But he saw one of the familiar oil lamps in its bracket hanging to a side wall nearby. He lit the lamp, waited until the chimney had warmed up, then turned up the wick. The stronger sweep of lamplight informed him that this must be the room under the stage where players and musicians loafed and waited for cues to climb a short flight of stairs. Then they would either step out from the wings upon the stage or enter the pit just below the stage footlights where orchestral music was played. Two or three closed doors opened off this larger room. Sunset saw a star painted on one. With curiosity aroused, he opened this door and glanced inside. The lamp showed him that this was a dressing room, a narrow cold place like a goal with a rude table and chair in front of a large mirror. Here actors sat—the star of the show—to make up for their turns. He saw on the table, powder puffs, bits of false hair, sticks of grease paint indicating that one actress had been using this room when driven out by the fire alarm.

Sunset walked over slowly and examined the make-up kit on the table. One length of red grease paint—sticky stuff—reminded him of the natural Indian war paint which Doc had shown to him, the stuff that had rubbed off on the linen duster of the murdered drummer and Jack Coogan. Hematite of iron.

Then, right above him, Sunset heard the thumping of heels. He stared upward, finally decided that here he stood directly beneath the stage. Then, listening, he thought that he heard the faint sound of voices above him. He knew that he dared not use the lamp now to climb the stairway from cellar to stage or orchestra pit. Men of Firebank's bunch, perhaps Freddy himself, would be up there, carrying liquor from the annex room where a bar catered to the needs of the audience.

So in darkness, carefully packing the cocked Winchester, Sunset climbed the stairway, hesitated momentarily where a door led to his left, climbed two more steps. And found himself standing amidst painted shadowy scenery in a wing, staring out upon the brightly lighted stage of a murdered man's play house.

CHAPTER XXI

A SHOW WAS GOING ON. THE CURTAIN HAD gone up. Even the tin pan piano was plunking out a quickstep. But for a queer sort of show, a sort of orgy such as Nero might have held while Rome burned. Fred Firebank stood on the stage. He was the master of ceremonies, the chief comedian, for now there was a smile on his scorched and blistered face. A table had been pulled to the centre of the stage. Upon it had been placed an opened bottle of whisky with attendant pony glasses. And seated at the table, brightly lighted by the footlights, sat Dulcy Pringle. She still wore her silken gown but there were rents in it showing recent rough handling and black holes where sparks from the fire had been hastily beaten out.

She sat obediently in the chair, Sunset perceived, because she had been tied to it. She was an exhibit for the merciless eyes of the gangsters and their women who lolled out in the front, resting between spells of loading liquor as they awaited the return of the coach. And in this interval, Fred Firebank was making merry. The girl from Chicago was the butt of his rude joke. At every sally he made, the painted women in the dancing costumes, and the smoky men in the seats, raised their toady laughter and derisively applauded.

"She'd like to do a buck and wing dance for you, folks," said Freddy. "But she didn't have time to put on minstrel make-up. But maybe I can fix that." He turned to the table, bent and picked up a stick of grease paint. And strutting over the helpless girl, he daubed her face with sticky black cork. He stepped back to survey his work and the crowd laughed. "She don't seem in the mood tonight," he said, "but give me a week to work on her, and she'll be our top turn."

Sunset saw that Firebank had been too near the face of the fire. Some of his fluffy brown moustache had been scorched. But such a mighty rage now filled Sunset that he gave the fate of Firebank's whiskers but passing reflection. He snapped the Winchester to his shoulder and prepared to open fire.

But before he could shoot, a turn stepped upon the stage, breaking up Fred's act. A ghostly turn such as the Buckskin boss had never imagined could appear before his eyes. From the dark wings across from Sunset, a portly figure seemed to drift into sight. This figure was draped in white smeared with red and upon its head there was crushed down a black hat resembling a battered derby. And this apparition croaked as it appeared, "Firebank—why did you kill me? Me—Boston Charley. Firebank—*I know you. The grave holds no secrets. Frank Flarity, murderer of women!*"

Firebank dropped his stick of black cork. He veered away from the ghost of Boston Charley, thrusting his hand under his scorched coat. Out in front, a dead silence fell upon the audience. No laughing or applauding now. All there knew that a fat detective from Boston lay murdered in the dugout of Doc. A drummer who had worn a white linen duster and a derby hat.

"No," gasped Firebank. "No—" But he was a gambler, and in all gamblers there runs a deep streak of superstition. He didn't believe in ghosts, but what was this horrible thing that now appeared? His eyes were distracted. And while his gaze was upon the spook, Sunset jumped out on the stage with rifle at the ready. "Not a man move!" he shouted.

Firebank whirled with a curse, drawing a hideout gun. But Dulcy, thrusting her slippers down on the floor, knocked over her chair and tumbled against Firebank's braced legs upsetting him. As he went down, unable to use his gun, Sunset sprang upon him like a tiger. There on the stage he wreaked vengeance with hard fists upon the face and body of Fred Firebank. All the while in strange silence for never a sound came from the audience. It was not until he arose from the whimpering thing at his feet that he saw old Jake standing in the rear of the theatre with the buffalo gun held ominously ready for a throwdown.

"Standing room only, folks," chanted Jake. "Just keep what seats you got unless you want a lead-nosed ticket to the balcony from my ol' buff'ler gun!"

The coach returned. In trooped the whisky handlers to be met by the guns of Jake and Sunset. A sullen crew was mustered, the battered form of Firebank carried out to the waiting coach. Doc, still arrayed in the dingy white table cover and battered black hat he had found down in the dressing room—and liberally plastered with red lipstick to indicate the blood of a murdered man—walked at one side of Dulcy and Sunset at the other as the two escorted the girl to the coach. There they stood on guard while Jake climbed to the high seat and then Sunset told Dulcy, bowing, "Your coach awaits, my dear!"

"You—where'll you ride?"

"Outside to whip for Jake. We don't aim to have

the mob stop us between here and the stage office. Doc'll ride inside with you and Freddy."

And so it was. Lines of firefighters along the street were suddenly alarmed by the thunder of wheels and the drumming of hoofs as the coach rolled past them with a whiskered old man on the box yelling encouragement to his wheelers, and a red-headed youth snapping the encouraging whip.

"Dang me," growled Old Man Smith, turning to look and wiping the soot from his eyes, "dang me if that wasn't Jake and that law man from Piute."

The coach snapped around a corner of the office and turned into the alley before the alarm could spread through the Buckskinners. The alarm that the men they blamed for setting the town on fire were now at large and had captured Firebank's whisky caravan.

Inside the office, men worked hurriedly toting the six kegs of powder, plenty of fuse, tools, such as picks and shovels, from the company's stores out to the coach. Then the final splitup was made. Sunset told his girl that he would ride with Doc, Jake, and the agent, up to the reservoir. She and Lonesome Luke would remain here in the locked office to stand guard over Mildred and Firebank.

Dulcy clung to Sunset. "You can't go," she whispered. "I thought I'd never see you again when they hauled me up to that horrible place."

"I'll come back," promised Sunset. He grinned and bent over her. "I don't mind black grease paint," he went on, and kissed her on the lips.

They barred the doors after the coach had clattered off, rumbling up the alley. This narrow aisle required careful driving but old Jake was equal to the task.

The driver's blood was up. His horses knew his voice and responded eagerly, even when they whirled away from town and breasted the steep little hill on top of which had been built the reservoir.

Water lapped around the headgate when they reached the spot they had chosen for the final blast in Buckskin. Powder kegs were hurriedly rolled from the coach. Deep holes were coyoted in the muck and sod on both sides of the wooden headgate which controlled water that ran into the ditch built for the use of the miners.

"Of course," panted Sunset, "if this thing works out, that flood'll wash out some of the best gold claims along the creek."

Doc flung down a muddy shovel. "Let 'er wash," he gasped. "Buckskin was a good little old camp. The gold never did her much good." He watched the stage agent run out lengths of fuse from the coach to the powder kegs mudded in around the headgate. "Give us plenty time to get rollin'," he advised the man, "before she lets go."

The fuse was sputtering, running rapidly toward the powder charges in the dam when the Buckskin rescue party got underway in the coach. Jake steered an angling course hopeful that they would not be caught in the main tidal wave that they hoped would come rolling and booming down the hill when the powder let go.

Jake kicked off the brake as the coach plunged and tossed its way down the hill. He yelled and shouted at his team, galloping desperately to avoid being overtaken by the runaway vehicle. Beside him, Sunset plied the whip. Doc and the agent clung to the inside of the coach, ready at any instant to jump for their lives if the wheels struck a rock and overturned the whole load.

Down in the main camp, a contingent of Buckskinners arrived at the stage office, forgetful for a moment of the dangerous fire still threatening theatre and hotel. Old Man Smith's heart wasn't in it but some of the men had heard him shout that Sunset had ridden the coach down here. Now they battered on the office door, demanding anew that Sunset surrender. The hoarse voice of Lonesome Luke warned them to be gone or he'd open fire. The mobsters could not know that Luke had staggered up from a bunk to offer the challenge. That two pale women crouched at the front windows with guns in their hands preparing for desperate resistance. And in the shadowy rear of the room, battered Fred Firebank stirred, sat up, and began to inch his way toward the centre table.

Here had been set out rolls of lint for the bandaging of Luke, a basin of warm water. Firebank was so maimed and beaten, so stunned, that Sunset had not waited to tie him up. He had stripped away the hide-out gun, laid it on the table, and kicked Firebank into the dark corner.

Now Firebank, still half senseless, raised and felt for the gun which glittered in the light of the dim lamp on the table; felt with groping hands, while Luke and the two women watched the front street where the mob had gathered.

Then came the usual battering attack. A yielding of the door. Luke broke out a window. He steadied his arm on the sill and began to shoot.

As though in answer to the blazing of his gun, a volley crashed at the lower end of the street. The mob whirled to face this new attack. Saw horsemen dashing toward them, flashing guns from which bloomed smoke and the yellow muzzle burst blossoms. The mobsters turned and ran.

Three horses were freed on the dead run. Three horsemen beat on the door. They were the real Boston Charley, Rattlesnake Bill, and the cook, Yum. Dulcy unbarred the door. They broke in just in time for Rattlesnake Bill to leap across the room and wrest the gun from the hand of Fred Firebank. And that brought a surprised yell from Bill as he stared at the gun.

"The derringer," he shouted, "with the gold ace of spades in the stock! The gun that creased me when I shot Mose DeBose."

Down Main Street roared the coach with Jake and Sunset whooping above thunder of hoofs and the rattle of wheels. A new war cry for Buckskin.

"Run for your lives! Flood comin'! *Hit for the high ground*!"

Wham! Off toward the east a mighty thudding roar sounded. A bright yellow flash flooded over the faint pink of coming dawn. Then *Whoom*! as a second charge exploded.

Buckskinners heard and ran in a mad delirium. They had thought before of saving their whisky but now they ran to save their hides.

Down from the huge gap, torn in the dam, swept a wall of frothy yellow water. Once it had cascaded down the hill and burst out into the wider space occupied by the town, it lost much of its original force. But there was enough water in town that blazing dawn to reach the neck of a man in the theatre and come up to the knees of a Buckskinner in the stage office. There was enough of the water, too, to spread out and save what remained of the camp.

The old sheriff and his contingent from Piute rode in later. But it was all over then. The election had been held and Doc was now mayor. With his assayer's scales he had demonstrated that the two bullets, one from the head of Hilda Beddows and the other fired into his cabin by Firebank, had both come from Firebank's hideout derringer, the thirty-two calibre derringer adorned with the ace of spades. Mildred had also produced the letter from her hat, from where she had hidden it behind the red bird, which described Frank Flarity as having a small blue scar on his face. This letter had been written by the murdered woman, Hilda, shortly after her wedding. Dulcy had disclosed that she had searched Firebank's room, discovered red make-up, and also a chunk of hematite of iron with which he pinkened his cheeks to hide the blue scar. As for the fluffy moustache, false, too, and most of it burned off Freddy's pink face by the fire.

Freddy would return to be hanged in good old Boston, the fat detective who had learned to ride a horse vowed. The Laramie law would favour Bill's statement that he had fired in self-defence. Mildred would return to the east to claim her inheritance. And Luke, arm in sling, would go with her. But Dulcy Pringle—she smiled upon Sunset McGee. "I like it out here," she said softly.

"Buckskin or bust!" sang Sunset, and echoed the slogan with a good hearty kiss that jarred Dulcy to the toes of her scorched slippers.

ZANE GREY'S FAMOUS CHARACTERS LIVE ON IN LEISURE'S ACTION-PACKED WESTERN SERIES BY HIS SON, ROMER ZANE GREY

2041-6	ZANE GREY'S LARAMIE NELSON: THE OTHER SIDE OF THE CANYON	$2.75
2082-3	ZANE GREY'S BUCK DUANE: RIDER OF DISTANT TRAILS	$2.75
2098-X	ZANE GREY'S ARIZONA AMES: GUN TROUBLE IN TONTO BASIN	$2.75
2116-1	ZANE GREY'S LARAMIE NELSON: THE LAWLESS LAND	$2.75
2136-6	ZANE GREY'S BUCK DUANE: KING OF THE RANGE	$2.75
2158-7	ZANE GREY'S ARIZONA AMES: KING OF THE OUTLAW HORDE	$2.75
2192-7	ZANE GREY'S YAQUI: SIEGE AT FORLORN RIVER	$2.75
2213-3	ZANE GREY'S NEVADA JIM LACY: BEYOND THE MOGOLLON RIM	$2.75

MORE HARD-RIDING, STRAIGHT-SHOOTING WESTERN ADVENTURE FROM LEISURE BOOKS

2091-2	**THE OUTSIDE LAWMAN** Lee O. Miller	$2.25
2130-7	**VENGEANCE MOUNTAIN** R.C. House	$2.25
2149-8	**CANAVAN'S TRAIL** Burt and Budd Arthur	$2.25
2182-X	**BULLWHACKER** James D. Nichols	$2.25
2193-5	**VENGEANCE VALLEY** Allen Appel	$2.25
2204-4	**ENEMY IN SIGHT** Bill Bragg	$2.25
2233-8	**THE SUDDEN LAND** Dale Oldham	$2.25
2234-6	**CUTLER: MUSTANG** H.V. Elkin	$2.25
2243-5	**SHOWDOWN COUNTRY** Charlie Barstow	$2.25
2244-3	**PRAIRIE VENGEANCE** M.L. Warren	$2.25
2254-0	**RUSTLER'S BLOOD** David Everitt	$2.25
2263-X	**BROTHER GUN** Jack Slade	$2.25
2264-8	**CHASE A TALL SHADOW** John Ell	$2.25

Make the Most of Your Leisure Time with
LEISURE BOOKS

Please send me the following titles:

Quantity	Book Number	Price
_____	_____	_____
_____	_____	_____
_____	_____	_____
_____	_____	_____
_____	_____	_____

If out of stock on any of the above titles, please send me the alternate title(s) listed below:

_____	_____	_____
_____	_____	_____
_____	_____	_____
_____	_____	_____

Postage & Handling _____

Total Enclosed $_____

☐ Please send me a free catalog.

NAME _____
(please print)

ADDRESS _____

CITY _____ STATE _____ ZIP _____

Please include $1.00 shipping and handling for the first book ordered and 25¢ for each book thereafter in the same order. All orders are shipped within approximately 4 weeks via postal service book rate. PAYMENT MUST ACCOMPANY ALL ORDERS.*

*Canadian orders must be paid in US dollars payable through a New York banking facility.

Mail coupon to: **Dorchester Publishing Co., Inc.**
6 East 39 Street, Suite 900
New York, NY 10016
Att: ORDER DEPT.